PENGUIN TWENTIETH-CENTURY CLASSICS

DEATH IN MIDSUMMER AND OTHER STORIES

Yukio Mishima was born in Tokyo in 192[illegible] [illegible]n he graduated from the Peers' Sch[illegible] [illegible]d a citation from the E[illegible] [illegible]our stud[illegible]nt. He then atte[illegible] [illegible]ial University School of Jurisprudenc[illegible] [illegible], he became a prolific write[illegible] [illegible], whose works include some fifteen novels [illegible] of which have been made into films), thirty-three plays, two travel books, numerous essays and countless short stories. Among his books published in England are *After the Banquet*, *Confessions of a Mask*, *Forbidden Colours* and *The Sailor Who Fell from Grace with the Sea*. *The Sound of Waves*, published in Japan under the title *Shiosai*, won the 1954 Shinchosha literary prize.

Mishima revered and mastered the martial arts of Japan. He was a devotee of body-building exercises and also accomplished in the arts of *kendo* and *karate*. He always firmly upheld the traditions of Japan's imperial past – a legacy from his samurai forbears – and believed that these values were being eroded by Western materialism.

On 25 November 1970, at the peak of his brilliant literary career, he astonished the world by committing ritual suicide, or *hara-kiri*, by disembowelment. Mishima had written much about suicide and early death and often expressed the wish to die young. His last work was the tetralogy, *The Sea of Fertility* which is published by Penguin. This comprises *Spring Snow*, *Runaway Horses*, *The Temple of Dawn* (in two parts) and *The Decay of the Angel* and was finally completed on the morning before his death. Just before his suicide he wrote to friends that he felt empty, having put everything he thought or felt about life into this mammoth undertaking, later hailed as a masterpiece. His writing has been widely acclaimed, compared to that of Proust, Gide and Sartre, and Arthur Miller once said of him that 'He had the economy of means to create enormous myths – his novels are compressed visions.'

[illegible] School in 1944 he received [illegible] from the Emperor as the highest honour student [illegible] attended the Tokyo Imperial University School of [illegible] until 1947. Starting in his teens, [illegible]

[illegible]

Yukio Mishima

Death in Midsummer

and Other Stories

Penguin Books
in association with Martin Secker & Warburg Ltd

PENGUIN BOOKS

Published by the Penguin Group
Penguin Books Ltd, 27 Wrights Lane, London W8 5TZ, England
Viking Penguin, a division of Penguin Books USA Inc.
375 Hudson Street, New York, New York 10014, USA
Penguin Books Australia Ltd, Ringwood, Victoria, Australia
Penguin Books Canada Ltd, 2801 John Street, Markham, Ontario, Canada L3R 1B4
Penguin Books (NZ) Ltd, 182–190 Wairau Road, Auckland 10, New Zealand

Penguin Books Ltd, Registered Offices: Harmondsworth, Middlesex, England

First published in the USA by New Directions 1966
Published in Great Britain by Martin Secker & Warburg Ltd 1967
Published in Penguin Books 1971
10 9 8 7

Printed in England by Clays Ltd, St Ives plc
Set in Intertype Times

Some of these stories have appeared previously in *Cosmopolitan*, *Esquire*, *Harper's Bazaar*, *Japan Quarterly*, and *Today's Japan*. 'The Priest of Shiga Temple and His Love' was published in the UNESCO collection *Modern Japanese Stories* by Eyre & Spottiswoode

To Philippe and Pauline de Rothschild

Contents

Death in Midsummer

La mort . . . nous affecte plus profondément sous le règne pompeux de l'été.

Baudelaire: Les Paradis Artificiels

A. Beach, near the southern tip of the Izu Peninsula, is still unspoiled for sea bathing. The sea bottom is pitted and uneven, it is true, and the surf is a little rough; but the water is clean, the slope out to sea is gentle, and conditions are on the whole good for swimming. Largely because it is so out of the way, A. Beach has none of the noise and dirt of resorts nearer Tokyo. It is a two-hour bus ride from Itō.

Almost the only inn is the Eirakusō, which also has cottages to rent. There are only one or two of the shabby refreshment stands that clutter most beaches in summer. The sand is rich and white, and half-way down the beach a rock, surmounted by pines, crouches over the sea almost as if it were the work of a landscape gardener. At high tide it lies half under water.

And the view is beautiful. When the west wind blows the mists from the sea, the islands off shore come in sight, Ōshima near at hand and Toshima farther off, and between them a little triangular island called Utoneshima. Beyond the headland of Nanago lies Cape Sakai, a part of the same mountain mass, throwing its roots deep into the sea; and beyond that the cape known as the Dragon Palace of Yatsu, and Cape Tsumeki, on the southern tip of which a lighthouse beam revolves each night.

In her room at the Eirakusō Tomoko Ikuta was taking a nap. She was the mother of three children, though one would never have suspected it to look at the sleeping figure. The knees showed under the one-piece dress, just a little short, of light salmon-pink linen. The plump arms, the unworn face, and the slightly curled lips gave off a girl-like freshness. Perspiration had come out on the forehead and in the hollows beside the nose. Flies buzzed dully, and the air was like the inside of a heated metal dome. The salmon linen rose and fell so slightly that it seemed the embodiment of the heavy, windless afternoon.

Most of the other guests were down on the beach. Tomoko's room was on the second floor. Below her window was a white swing for children. There were chairs on the lawn, as well as tables and a peg for quoits. The quoits lay scattered over the lawn. No one was in sight, and the buzzing of an occasional bee was drowned out by the waves beyond the hedge. The pines came immediately up to the hedge, and gave way beyond to the sand and the surf. A stream passed under the inn. It formed a pool before spilling into the ocean, and fourteen or fifteen geese would splash and honk most indelicately as they fed there every afternoon.

Tomoko had two sons, Kiyoo and Katsuo, who were six and three, and a daughter, Keiko, who was five. All three were down on the beach with Yasue, Tomoko's sister-in-law. Tomoko felt no qualms about asking Yasue to take care of the children while she had a nap herself.

Yasue was an old maid. In need of help after Kiyoo was born, Tomoko had consulted her husband and decided to invite Yasue in from the provinces. There was no real reason why Yasue had remained unmarried. She was not particularly alluring, indeed, but then neither was she homely. She had declined proposal after proposal, until she was past the age for marrying. Much taken with the idea of following her brother to Tokyo, she leaped at Tomoko's invitation. Her family had plans for marrying her off to a provincial notable.

Yasue was far from quick, but she was very good-natured. She addressed Tomoko, younger than she, as an older sister, and was always careful to defer to her. The Kanazawa accent had almost disappeared. Besides helping with the children and the housework, Yasue went to sewing school and made clothes for herself, of course, and for Tomoko and the children too. She would take out her notebook and sketch new fashions in downtown shop windows, and sometimes she would find a shopgirl glaring at her and even reprimanding her.

She was down on the beach in a stylish green bathing suit. This alone she had not made – it was from a department store.

Very proud of her fair north-country skin, she showed hardly a trace of sunburn. She always hurried from the water back to her umbrella. The children were at the edge of the water building a sand castle, and Yasue amused herself by dripping the watery sand on her white leg. The sand, immediately dry, fell into a dark pattern, sparkling with tiny shell fragments. Yasue hastily brushed at it, as if from a sudden fear that it would not wash off. A half-transparent little insect jumped from the sand and scurried away.

Stretching her legs and leaning back on her hands, Yasue looked out to sea. Great cloud masses boiled up, immense in their quiet majesty. They seemed to drink up all the noise below, even the sound of the sea.

It was the height of summer and there was anger in the rays of the sun.

The children were tired of the sand castle. They ran off kicking up the water in the shallows. Startled from the safe little private world into which she had slipped, Yasue ran after them.

But they did nothing dangerous. They were afraid of the roar of the waves. There was a gentle eddy beyond the line where the waves fell back. Kiyoo and Keiko, hand in hand, stood waist-deep in the water, their eyes sparkling as they braced against the water and felt the sand at the soles of their feet.

'Like someone's pulling,' said Kiyoo to his sister.

Yasue came up beside them and warned them not to go in any deeper. She pointed at Katsuo. They shouldn't leave him there alone, they should go up and play with him. But they paid no attention to her. They stood hand in hand, smiling happily at each other. They had a secret all their own, the feel of the sand as it pulled away from their feet.

Yasue was afraid of the sun. She looked at her shoulder and her breasts, and she thought of the snow in Kanazawa. She gave herself a little pinch high on the breast. She smiled at the warmth. The nails were a little long and there was sand under them – she would have to cut them when she got back to her room.

She no longer saw Kiyoo and Keiko. They must have gone back up on the beach.

But Katsuo was alone. His face was strangely twisted, and he was pointing towards her.

Her heart beat violently. She looked into the water at her feet. It was receding again, and in the foam some two yards away a little brown body was rolling over and over. She caught a glimpse of Kiyoo's dark blue swimming trunks.

Her heart beat still more violently. She moved towards the body as if she were fighting her way out of a corner. A wave came farther in than usual, loomed over her, broke before her eyes. It struck her square in the breast. She fell back into the water. She had had a heart attack.

Katsuo began crying, and a youth ran up from near by. Several others ran out through the shallows. The water leaped up around their naked black bodies.

Two or three saw the fall. They thought nothing about it. She would get up again. But at such times there is always a premonition, and as they ran up it half seemed to them that there had been something wrong with that fall.

Yasue was carried up to the scorching sand. Her eyes were open and her teeth clenched, and she seemed to be gazing in horror at something planted squarely in front of her. One of the men felt her pulse. There was none.

'She's staying at the Eirakusō.' Someone recognized her.

The manager of the inn must be called. A boy from the village, determined not to let anyone steal this proud work from him, ran over the hot sand at top speed.

The manager came. He was about forty. He had on shorts and a sagging T-shirt, and, worn through here and there, a woollen band over his stomach. He argued that Yasue should be given first aid at the inn. Someone objected. Without waiting for the argument to be settled, two young men picked Yasue up and started to carry her off. The wet sand where she had lain showed the outlines of a human form.

Katsuo followed wailing after them. Someone noticed and picked him up.

Tomoko was aroused from her nap. The manager, well

trained for his work, shook her gently. She lifted her head and asked what was wrong.

'The lady named Yasue . . .'

'Has something happened to Yasue?'

'We've given her first aid, and the doctor will be here in no time.'

Tomoko jumped up and hurried out with the manager. Yasue lay on the lawn beside the swing, and a near-naked man knelt straddling her. He was giving her artificial respiration. To one side was a heap of straw and broken-up orange crates, and two men were doing their best to start a fire. The flames would immediately give way to smoke. The wood was still wet from a storm the night before. A third man fanned away the smoke as it curled towards Yasue's face.

Her head thrown back, Yasue looked for all the world as if she were breathing. In the sunlight that filtered through the trees, sweat glistened on the dark back of the man astride her. The white legs, stretched out on the grass, were plump and chalky. They seemed apathetic, quite divorced from the struggle going on above.

Tomoko knelt in the grass.

'Yasue! Yasue!'

Would they save Yasue? Why had it happened? What could she say to her husband? Weeping and incoherent, she jumped from question to question. Presently she turned sharply to the men around her. Where were the children?

'Look. Your mother's here.' A middle-aged fisherman held a frightened Katsuo in his arms. Tomoko glanced at the boy, and nodded her thanks to the fisherman.

The doctor came and continued the artificial respiration. Her cheeks burning in the firelight, Tomoko hardly knew what she was thinking. An ant crawled across Yasue's face. Tomoko crushed it and flicked it away. Another ant crawled from the shaking hair up towards the ear. Tomoko crushed it too. Crushing ants became her job.

The artificial respiration went on for four hours. There were finally signs that *rigor mortis* was setting in, and the doctor gave up. The body was covered with a sheet and carried to the second floor. The room was dark. A man left the body and ran ahead to switch on the light.

Exhausted, Tomoko felt a sort of sweet emptiness come over her. She was not sad. She thought of the children.

'The children?'

'Down in the play room with Gengo.'

'All three of them?'

'All three?' The men looked at each other.

Tomoko pushed them aside and ran downstairs. The fisherman, Gengo, in a cotton kimono, sat on the sofa going over a picture book with Katsuo, who had on an adult's shirt over his swimming-trunks. Katsuo's mind was on something else. He was not looking at the book.

As Tomoko came in, the guests, who knew of the tragedy, stopped fanning themselves and looked at her.

She almost threw herself on Katsuo.

'Kiyoo and Keiko?' she asked harshly.

Katsuo looked up at her timidly. 'Kiyoo ... Keiko ... all bubbles.' He began sobbing.

Tomoko ran down to the beach in her bare feet. The pine needles stabbed at her as she went through the grove. The tide had come in, and she had to climb over the rock to the bathing-beach. The sand stretched out white below her. She could see far into the dusk. One umbrella, checkered yellow and white, had been left behind. It was her own.

The others overtook her on the beach. She was running recklessly through the surf. When they tried to stop her, she brushed them irritably away.

'Don't you see? There are two children out there.'

Many had not heard what Gengo had had to say. They thought Tomoko was mad.

It hardly seemed possible that no one had thought of the other two children in the whole four hours they were looking after Yasue. The people at the inn were used to seeing the three children together. And however upset their mother might be, it was strange that no warning came to her of the death of her two children.

Sometimes, however, such an incident sets in motion a sort of group psychology that lets only the same simple thoughts come to everyone. It is not easy to stand outside. It is not easy to register dissent. Aroused from her afternoon nap, Tomoko had simply taken over what the others passed on to her, and had not thought to question.

All that night there were bonfires some yards apart up and down the beach. Every thirty minutes the young men would dive to look for the bodies. Tomoko was on the beach with them. She could not sleep, partly no doubt because she had slept too long that afternoon.

On the advice of the constabulary, the nets were not set out the following morning.

The sun came up over the headland to the left of the beach, and the morning breeze struck Tomoko's face. She had dreaded the daylight. It seemed to her that with the daylight the whole of the truth must come out, and the tragedy would for the first time become real.

'Don't you think you should get some rest?' said one of the older men. 'We'll call you if we find anything. You can leave everything to us.'

'Please do, please do,' said the inn manager, red-eyed from lack of sleep. 'You've had enough bad luck. What will your husband do if you take sick yourself?'

Tomoko was afraid to see her husband. Seeing him would be like meeting a trial judge. But she would have to see him. The time was coming near – yet another disaster was coming near, it seemed to her.

Presently she summoned up her courage to send a telegram. It gave her an excuse to leave the beach. She had begun to feel that the direction of all the divers had been turned over to her.

She looked back as she walked off. The sea was quiet. A silvery light flashed in near the shore. Fish were jumping. They seemed quite intoxicated with delight. It was unfair that Tomoko should be so unhappy.

Her husband, Masaru Ikuta, was thirty-five. A graduate of the Tokyo University of Foreign Studies, he had gone to work for an American company before the war. His English was good, and he knew his business – he was abler than his silent manner suggested. Now the manager of the Japanese office of an American automobile company, he had the use of a company automobile, half as advertising, and he made 150,000 yen a month. He also had ways of appropriating certain secret funds for himself, and Tomoko and Yasue, with a maid to take care of the children, lived in comfort and security. There was no pressing need to cut the family down by three.

Tomoko sent a telegram because she did not want to talk to Masaru over the telephone. As was the custom in the suburbs, the post office telephoned the message when it arrived, and the call came just as Masaru was about to leave for work. Thinking it a routine business call, he calmly picked up the telephone.

'We have a rush telegram from A. Beach,' said the woman in the post office. Masaru began to feel uneasy. 'I'll read it to you. Are you ready? "YASUE DEAD. KIYOO AND KEIKO MISSING. TOMOKO."'

'Would you read it again, please?'

It sounded the same the second time: 'YASUE DEAD. KIYOO AND KEIKO MISSING. TOMOKO.' Masaru was angry. It was as though, for no reason he could think of, he had suddenly received notice of his dismissal.

He immediately telephoned the office and said he would not be in. He thought he might drive to A. Beach. But the road was long and dangerous, and he had no confidence that he could drive it, upset as he was. As a matter of fact he had recently had an accident. He decided to take a train to Itō, and a taxi from there.

The process by which the unforeseen event works its way into a man's consciousness is a strange and subtle one. Masaru, who set out without even knowing the nature of the incident, was careful to take a good supply of money with him. Incidents required money.

He took a taxi to Tokyo station. He felt nothing he could really call emotion. He felt rather what a detective might feel on his way to the scene of a crime. Plunged less in speculation than in deduction, he quivered with curiosity to know more about the incident that involved him so deeply.

She could have telephoned. She was afraid to talk to me. With a husband's intuition, he sensed the truth. But in any case the first problem is to go and see for myself.

He looked out of the window as they came near the heart of the city. The sun of the midsummer morning was even more blinding because of the white-shirted crowds. The trees along the road cast deep shadows directly downwards, and at the entrance to a hotel the gaudy red-and-white awning was taut, as if the sunlight were a heavy metal. The newly dug earth where the street was being repaired was already dry and dusty.

The world around him was quite as it had always been. Nothing had happened, and if he tried he could believe that nothing had happened even to him. A childish annoyance came over him. In an unknown place, an incident with which he had had nothing to do had cut him off from the world.

Among all these passengers none was so unfortunate as he. The thought seemed to put him on a level above or a level below the ordinary Masaru, he did not know which. He was someone special. Someone apart.

No doubt a man with a large birthmark on his back sometimes feels the urge to call out: 'Listen, everyone. You don't know it, but I have a big, purple birthmark on my back.'

And Masaru wanted to shout at the other passengers: 'Listen, everybody. You don't know it, but I have just lost my sister and two of my three children.'

His courage left him. If only the children were safe. . . . He began trying to think of other ways to interpret the telegram. Possibly Tomoko, distraught over Yasue's death, had assumed that the children were dead when they had only lost their way. Might not a second telegram be waiting at the house even now? Masaru was quite taken up with his own feelings, as if the incident itself were less important than his reaction to it. He regretted that he had not called the Eirakusō immediately.

The plaza in front of Itō station was brilliant in the midsummer sun. Beside the taxi stand was a little office, no bigger than a police box. The sunlight inside it was merciless, and the edges of the dispatch sheets on the walls were brown and curled.

'How much to A. Beach?'

'Two thousand yen.' The man wore a driver's cap, and had a towel around his neck. 'If you're in no hurry, you can save money going by bus. It leaves in five minutes,' he added, either out of kindness or because the trip seemed too much of an effort.

'I'm in a hurry. Someone in my family has just died there.'

'Oh? You're related to the people who drowned at A. Beach? That's too bad. Two children and a woman all at once, they say.'

Masaru felt dizzy under the blazing sun. He did not say another word to the driver until the taxi reached A. Beach.

There was no particularly distinguished scenery along the way. At first the taxi climbed up one dusty mountain and down the next, and the sea was rarely in sight. When they passed another car along a narrow stretch of road, branches slapped at the half-open window like startled birds, and dropped dirt and sand rudely on Masaru's carefully pressed trousers.

Masaru could not decide how to face his wife. He was not sure that there was such a thing as a 'natural approach' when none of the emotions he had ready seemed to fit. Perhaps the unnatural was in fact natural.

The taxi pulled through the darkened old gate of the Eirakusō. As it came up the driveway, the manager ran out with a clattering of wooden sandals. Masaru automatically reached for his wallet.

'I'm Ikuta.'

'A terrible thing,' said the manager, bowing deeply. After paying the driver, Masaru thanked the manager and gave him a thousand-yen note.

Tomoko and Katsuo were in a room adjoining the room where Yasue's coffin lay. The body was packed in dry ice ordered from Itō, and would be cremated now that Masaru had arrived.

Masaru stepped ahead of the manager and opened the door. Tomoko, who had lain down for a nap, jumped up at the sound. She had not been asleep.

Her hair was tangled and she had on a wrinkled cotton kimono. Like a convicted criminal, she pulled the kimono together and knelt meekly before him. Her motions were astonishingly quick, as though she had planned them in advance. She stole a glance at her husband and collapsed in tears.

He did not want the manager to see him lay a comforting hand on her shoulder. That would be worse than having the most intimate bedroom secrets spied on. Masaru took off his coat and looked for a place to hang it.

Tomoko noticed. Taking a blue hanger from the lintel, she hung up the sweaty coat for him. Masaru sat down beside Katsuo, who had been awakened by his mother's weeping and lay looking up at them. The child, on his knees, was as unresisting as a doll. How can children be so small? he wondered. It was almost as if he were holding a toy.

Tomoko knelt weeping in a corner of the room.

'It was all my fault,' she said. Those were the words Masaru most wanted to hear.

Behind them, the manager too was in tears. 'I know it's no business of mine, sir, but please don't blame Mrs Ikuta. It happened while she was taking a nap, and through no fault of hers.'

Masaru felt as if he had heard or read of all this somewhere.

'I understand, I understand.'

Obeying the rules, he stood up with the child in his arms, and, going over to his wife, laid his hand gently on her shoulder. The gesture came easily.

Tomoko wept even more bitterly.

The two bodies were found the next day. The constabulary, diving all up and down the beach, finally found them under the headland. Sea creatures had nibbled at them, and there were two or three creatures up each little nostril.

Such incidents of course go far beyond the dictates of custom, and yet at no time are people more bound to follow custom. Tomoko and Masaru forgot none of the responses and the return gifts custom demanded.

A death is always a problem in administration. They were frantically busy administering. One might say that Masaru in particular, as head of the family, had almost no time for sorrow. As for Katsuo, it seemed to him that one festival day succeeded another, with the adults all playing parts.

In any case, they steered their way through the whole complex affair. The funeral offerings came to a considerable sum. Funeral offerings are always larger when the head of the family, who can still provide, is a survivor than when it is his funeral.

Both Masaru and Tomoko were somehow braced for what had to be done. Tomoko did not understand how this almost insane grief and this careful attention to detail could exist side by side. And it was surprising too that she could eat so heavily without even noticing the taste.

What she dreaded most was having to see Masaru's parents. They arrived from Kanazawa in time for the funeral. 'It was all my fault,' she forced herself to say again, and by way of compensation she turned to her own parents.

'But who should they feel sorriest for? Haven't I just lost two children? There they all are, accusing me. They put the whole blame on me, and I have to apologize to them. They all look at me as if I were the absent-minded maid who dropped the baby in the river. But wasn't it Yasue? Yasue is lucky she's dead. Why can't they see who's been hurt? I'm a mother who has just lost two children.'

'You're being unfair. Who is accusing you? Wasn't his mother in tears when she said she felt sorrier for you than anyone?'

'She was just saying so.'

Tomoko was thoroughly dissatisfied. She felt like one demoted and condemned to obscurity, one whose real merit went unnoticed. It seemed to her that such intense sorrows should bring special privileges with them, extraordinary privileges. Some of the dissatisfaction was with herself, apologizing thus abjectly to her mother-in-law. It was to her mother that she went running when her irritation, like an itching rash all over her body, got the better of her.

She did not know it, but she was actually in despair at the poverty of human emotions. Was it not irrational that there was nothing to do except weep when ten people died, just as one wept for but a single person?

Tomoko wondered why she did not collapse. It seemed strange that she did not collapse, standing there in mourning for more than an hour in the midsummer heat. Sometimes she felt a little faint, and what saved her each time was a fresh start of horror at death. 'I'm a stronger person than I thought,' she said, turning a tearful face to her mother.

Talking with his parents of Yasue, Masaru shed tears for the sister who had thus died an old maid, and Tomoko felt a touch of resentment towards him too.

'Who is more important to him, Yasue or the children?' she wanted to ask.

There was no doubt that she was tense and ready. She could not sleep on the night of the wake, even though she knew she should. And yet she had not even a suggestion of a headache. Her mind was clear and taut.

Callers would worry over her, and sometimes she answered them roughly: 'You needn't think about me. It makes no difference whether I am alive or dead.'

Thoughts of suicide and insanity left her. Katsuo would be for a time the best reason why she should go on living. But sometimes she thought that it was only a failure of courage, or perhaps passion gone limp, whatever it was that made her think, as she looked at Katsuo being read to by the mourning women, how good it was that she had not killed herself. On such nights she would lie in her husband's arms and, turning eyes as wide as a rabbit's on the circle of light from the bed lamp, repeat over and over again, like one pleading a case: 'I was wrong. It was my fault. I should have known from the start that it was a mistake to leave the three children with Yasue.'

The voice was as hollow as a voice testing a mountain echo.

Masaru knew what this obsessive sense of responsibility

meant. She was waiting for some sort of punishment. She was greedy for it, one might say.

After the fourteenth-day services, life returned to normal. People urged them to go off somewhere for a rest, but mountain and seashore both terrified Tomoko. She was convinced that misfortunes never came alone.

One evening late in summer, Tomoko went into the city with Katsuo. She was to meet her husband for dinner when he finished work.

There was nothing Katsuo could not have. Both his mother and his father were almost uncomfortably gentle. They handled him as they would a glass doll, and it was a great undertaking even to see him across a street. His mother would glare at the cars and lorries stopped for a light, and dash across with his hand clutched in hers.

The last of the swimming suits in the store windows assailed her. She had to turn her eyes from a green bathing suit like Yasue's. Afterwards she wondered whether the mannequin had had a head. It seemed that it had not – and again that it had, and a face exactly like Yasue's dead face, the eyes closed in the wet, tangled hair. All the mannequins became drowned corpses.

If only summer would end. The very word 'summer' carried with it festering thoughts of death. And in the evening sun she felt a festering warmth.

Since it was still a little early, she took Katsuo into a department store. It was only a half-hour or so before closing time. Katsuo wanted to look at toys, and they went up to the third floor. They hurried past the beach playthings. Mothers were frantically going through a heap of marked-down bathing suits for children. One woman held a pair of dark-blue trunks high to the window, and the afternoon sun reflected from the buckle. Enthusiastically looking for a shroud, thought Tomoko.

When he had bought his blocks, Katsuo wanted to go up to the roof. The roof playground was cool. A fairly strong breeze from the harbour flapped at the awnings.

Tomoko looked through the wire netting at Kachidoki Bridge beyond the city, and at the Tsukishima docks and the cargo ships anchored in the bay.

Taking his hand from hers, Katsuo went over to the monkey cage. Tomoko stood over him. Possibly because of the wind, the monkey smell was strong. The monkey gazed at them with wrinkled forehead. As it moved from one branch to another, a hand carefully pressed to its hips, Tomoko could see at the side of the oldish little face a dirty ear with red veins showing through. She had never looked so carefully at an animal before.

Beside the cage was a pond. The fountain in the middle was turned off. There were beds of portulaca around the brick rim, on which a child about Katsuo's age was teetering precariously. His parents were nowhere in sight.

I hope he falls in. I hope he falls in and drowns.

Tomoko watched the uncertain legs. The child did not fall. When he had been once round, he noticed Tomoko's gaze and laughed proudly. Tomoko did not laugh. It was as if the child were making fun of her.

She took Katsuo by the hand and hurried down from the roof.

At dinner, Tomoko spoke after rather too long a silence: 'Aren't you quiet, though! And you don't seem the least bit sad.'

Startled, Masaru looked to see whether anyone had heard. 'You don't see? I'm only trying to cheer you up.'

'There's no need to do that.'

'So you say. But what about the effect on Katsuo?'

'I don't deserve to be a mother, anyway.'

And so the dinner was ruined.

Masaru tended more and more to retreat before his wife's sorrow. A man has work to do. He can distract himself with his work. Meanwhile Tomoko nursed the sorrow. Masaru had to face this monotonous sorrow when he came home, and so he began coming home later at night.

Tomoko phoned a maid who had worked for her long before and gave away all of Kiyoo's and Keiko's clothes and toys. The maid had children of about the same ages.

One morning Tomoko awoke a little later than usual. Masaru, who had been drinking again the night before, lay curled up on his side of the double bed. There was still a dank smell of liquor. The springs squeaked as he turned over in his sleep. Now that Katsuo was alone, she let him sleep in their second-floor bedroom, though she knew of course that it would be better not to. Through the white mosquito net over their own bed and the net over Katsuo's she looked at the child's sleeping face. He always wore a sort of pout when he slept.

Tomoko reached out of the mosquito net for the curtain cord. The roughness of the stiff cord in its hempen cover was pleasant against her sweaty hand. The curtain parted a little. The light struck the sandalwood-tree from below, so that the shadows piled on each other, and the wide clusters of leaves were even softer than usual. Sparrows were chirping noisily. Every morning they would wake up and start chattering to one another, and apparently they would then form a line and run up and down the gutter. The confused patter of little feet would go from one end of the gutter to the other and back again. Tomoko smiled as she listened.

It was a blessed morning. She had to feel that it was, for no reason at all. She lay quietly with her head still on the pillow. A feeling of happiness diffused itself through her whole body.

Suddenly she gasped. She knew why she was so happy. Last night for the first time she had not dreamed of the children. Every night she had dreamed of them, and last night she had not. She had had instead some pleasant, foolish little dream.

She had forgotten so soon, then – her heartlessness struck her as fearful. She wept tears of apology to the children's spirits. Masaru opened his eyes and looked at her. But he saw a sort of peace in the weeping, and not the usual anguish.

'You thought of them again?'

'Yes.' It seemed too much trouble to tell the truth.

But now that she had told a lie, she was annoyed that her husband did not weep with her. If she had seen tears in his eyes, she might have been able to believe her lie.

The forty-ninth-day services were over. Masaru bought a lot in the Tama Cemetery. These were the first deaths in his branch of the family, and the first graves. Yasue was charged with watching over the children on the Far Shore too: by agreement with the main family, her ashes were to be buried in the same lot.

Tomoko's fears came to seem groundless as the sadness only grew deeper. She went with Masaru and Katsuo to see the new cemetery lot. Already it was early autumn.

It was a beautiful day. The heat was leaving the high, clear sky.

Memory sometimes makes hours run side by side for us, or pile one on another. It played this strange trick on Tomoko twice in the course of the day. Perhaps, with the sky and the sunlight almost too clear, the edges of her subconscious too were somehow made half transparent.

Two months before the drownings, there had been that car accident. Masaru had not been hurt, of course, but after the drownings Tomoko never rode with him in the car when she took Katsuo out. Today Masaru too had to go by train.

They changed at M. for the little branch line to the cemetery. Masaru got off the train first with Katsuo. Held back in the crowd, Tomoko was able to get off only a second or two before the door closed. She heard a shrill whistle as the door slid shut behind her, and, almost screaming, she turned and tried to force it open again. She thought she had left Kiyoo and Keiko inside.

Masaru led her off by the arm. She looked at him defiantly, as if he were a detective arresting her. Coming to herself an instant later, she tried to explain what had happened – she must explain somehow. But the explanation only made Masaru uncomfortable. He thought she was acting.

Young Katsuo was delighted at the old-fashioned locomotive that took them to the cemetery. It had a high funnel, and it was wonderfully tall, as though on stilts. The wooden sill on which the engineer leaned his elbow might have been made of coal. The locomotive groaned and sighed and gnashed its teeth, and finally started off through the unexciting suburban market gardens.

Tomoko, who had never been to the Tama Cemetery before,

was astonished at its brightness. So wide a space, then, was given to the dead? The green lawns, the wide tree-lined avenues, the blue sky above, clear far into the distance. The city of the dead was cleaner and better ordered than the city of the living. She and her husband had had no cause to learn of cemeteries, but it did not seem unfortunate that they had now become qualified visitors. While neither of them especially thought about the matter, it seemed that the period of mourning, an unrelieved parade of the dark and the sinister, had brought them a sort of security, something stable, easy, pleasant even. They had become conditioned to death, and, as when people are conditioned to depravity, they had come to feel that life held nothing they need fear.

The lot was on the far side of the cemetery. Perspiring freely as they walked in from the gate, they looked curiously at Admiral T's grave, and laughed at a large, tasteless tombstone decorated with mirrors.

Tomoko listened to the subdued humming of the autumn cicadas, and smelled the incense and the cool, shady grass. 'What a nice place. They'll have room to play, and they won't be bored. I can't help thinking it will be good for them. Strange, isn't it?'

Katsuo was thirsty. There was a high brown tower at the crossroads. The circular steps at the base were stained from the leaking fountain in the centre. Several children, tired of chasing dragonflies, were noisily drinking water and squirting water at each other. Now and then a spray of water traced a thin rainbow through the air.

Katsuo was a child of action. He wanted a drink, and there was no help for it. Taking advantage of the fact that his mother was not holding his hand, he ran towards the steps. Where was he going? she called sharply. For a drink of water, he answered over his shoulder. She ran after him and took both his arms firmly from behind. 'That hurt,' he protested. He was frightened. Some terrible creature had pounced upon him from behind.

Tomoko knelt in the coarse gravel and turned him towards

her. He looked at his father, gazing in astonishment from beside a hedge some distance off.

'You are not to drink that water. We have some here.'

She began to unscrew the lid of the thermos flask on her knee.

They reached their bit of property. It was in a newly opened section of the cemetery behind rows of tombstones. Frail young box-trees were planted here and there, after a definite pattern, one could see if one looked carefully. The ashes had not yet been moved from the family temple, and there was no grave marker. There was only a roped-off bit of level land.

'And all three of them will be here together,' said Masaru.

The remark did little to Tomoko. How, she wondered, could facts be so completely improbable? For one child to drown in the ocean – that could happen, and no doubt anyone would accept it as a fact. But for three people to drown; that was ridiculous. And yet ten thousand was different again. There was something ridiculous about the excessive, and yet there was nothing ridiculous about a great natural catastrophe, or war. One death was somehow grave and solemn, as were a million deaths. The slightly excessive was different.

'Three of them. What nonsense! Three of them,' she said.

It was too large a number for one family, too small a number for society. And there were none of the social implications of death in battle or death at one's post. Selfish in her womanly way, she turned over and over again the riddle of this number. Masaru, the social being, had in the course of time come to note that it was convenient to see the matter as society saw it; they were in fact lucky that there were no social implications.

Back at the station, Tomoko fell victim again to that doubling up of time. They had to wait twenty minutes for the train. Katsuo wanted one of the toy badgers on sale in front of the station. The badgers, dangling from sticks, were of cotton wadding scorched a badger colour, to which were added eyes, ears, and tails.

'You can still buy these badgers!' exclaimed Tomoko.

'And children seem to like them as much as ever.'

'I had one when I was a child.'

Tomoko bought a badger from the old woman at the stall and gave it to Katsuo. And a moment later she caught herself looking around at the other stalls. She would have to buy something for Kiyoo and Keiko, who had been left at home.

'What is it?' asked Masaru.

'I wonder what's the matter with me. I was thinking I had to buy something for the others.' Tomoko raised her plump white arms and rubbed roughly with clenched fists at her eyes and temples. Her nostrils trembled as though she were about to weep.

'Go ahead and buy something. Buy something for them.' Masaru's tone was tense and almost pleading. 'We can put it on the altar.'

'No. They have to be alive.' Tomoko pressed her handkerchief to her nose. She was living, the others were dead. That was the great evil. How cruel it was to have to be alive.

She looked around her again: at the red flags hanging from the bars and restaurants in front of the station, at the gleaming white sections of granite piled high before the tombstone shops, at the yellowing paper-panelled doors on the second floors, at the roof tiles, at the blue sky, now darkening towards evening clear as porcelain. It was all so clear, so well defined. In the very cruelty of life was a deep peace, as of falling into a faint.

Autumn wore on, and the life of the family became day by day more tranquil. Not of course that grief was quite discarded. As Masaru saw his wife growing calmer, however, the joys of home and affection for Katsuo began to bring him back early from work; and even if, after Katsuo was in bed, the talk turned to what they both wanted not to talk of, they were able to find a sort of consolation in it.

The process by which so fearful an event could melt back into everyday life brought on a new sort of fear, mixed with shame, as if they had committed a crime that was finally to go undetected. The knowledge, always with them, that three people were missing from the family seemed at times to give a strange sense of fulfilment.

No one went mad, no one committed suicide. No one was even ill. The terrible event had passed and left scarcely a shadow. Tomoko came to feel bored. It was as if she were waiting for something.

They had long forbidden themselves plays and concerts, but Tomoko presently found excuses: such pleasures were in fact meant to comfort the grieving. A famous violinist from America was on a concert tour, and they had tickets. Katsuo was forced to stay at home, partly at least because Tomoko wanted to drive to the concert with her husband.

She was a long time getting ready. It took long to redo hair that had for months been left unattended. Her face in the mirror, when she was ready, was enough to bring back memories of long-forgotten pleasures. How to describe the pleasure of quite losing oneself in a mirror? She had forgotten what a delight a mirror could be – no doubt grief, with its stubborn insistence on the self, drew one away from such ecstasies.

She tried on kimono after kimono, finally choosing a lavish purple one and a brocade obi. Masaru, waiting behind the wheel of the car, was astonished at his beautiful wife.

People turned to look at her all up and down the lobby. Masaru was immensely pleased. It seemed to Tomoko herself, however, that no matter how beautiful people thought her, something would be lacking. There had been a time when she would have gone home quite satisfied after having attracted so much attention. This gnawing dissatisfaction, she told herself, must be the product of liveliness and gaiety that only emphasized how far from healed her grief was. But as a matter of fact it was only a recurrence of the vague dissatisfaction she had felt at not being treated as became a woman of sorrows.

The music had its effect on her, and she walked through the lobby with a sad expression on her face. She spoke to a friend. The expression seemed quite to suit the words of consolation the friend murmured. The friend introduced the young man with her. The young man knew nothing of Tomoko's sorrows and said nothing by way of consolation. His talk was of the most ordinary, including one or two lightly critical remarks about the music.

What a rude young man, thought Tomoko, looking at the shining head as it moved off through the crowd. He said nothing. And he must have seen how sad I was.

The young man was tall and stood out in the crowd. As he turned to one side, Tomoko saw the eyebrows and the laughing eyes, and a lock of hair straying down over the forehead. Only the top of the woman's head was visible.

Tomoko felt a stab of jealousy. Had she hoped to have from the young man something besides consolation, then – had she wanted other, rather special words? Her whole moral being quaked at the thought. She had to tell herself that this new suspicion was quite at odds with reason. She who had never once been dissatisfied with her husband.

'Are you thirsty?' asked Masaru, who had been speaking to a friend. 'There's an orangeade stand over there.'

People were sucking the orange liquid from tilted bottles. Tomoko looked over with the puzzled squint one so often sees on the nearsighted. She was not in the least thirsty. She remembered the day she had kept Katsuo from the fountain and had made him drink boiled water instead. Katsuo was not the only one in danger. There must be all sorts of little germs milling about in the orangeade.

She went slightly insane in her pursuit of pleasure. There was something vengeful in this feeling that she must have pleasure.

Not of course that she was tempted to be unfaithful to her husband. Wherever she went, she was with him or wanted to be.

Her conscience dwelt rather on the dead. Back from some amusement, she would look at the sleeping face of Katsuo, who had been put to bed early by the maid, and as she thought of the two dead children she would be quite overcome with remorse. Indeed the pursuit of pleasure became a sure way to stir up a pang of conscience.

Tomoko remarked suddenly that she wanted to take up sewing. This was not the first time Masaru had found it hard to follow the twists and jumps in a woman's thinking.

Tomoko began her sewing. Her pursuit of pleasure became less strenuous. She quietly looked about her, meaning to become the complete family woman. She felt that she was 'looking life square in the face'.

There were clear traces of neglect in her reappraised surroundings. She felt as if she had come back from a long trip. She would spend a whole day washing and a whole day putting things in order. The middle-aged maid had all her work snatched away from her.

Tomoko came on a pair of Kiyoo's shoes, and a little pair of light-blue felt slippers that had belonged to Keiko. Such relics would plunge her into meditation, and make her weep pleasant tears; but they all seemed tainted with bad luck. She telephoned a friend who was immersed in charities, and, feeling most elevated, gave everything to an orphanage, even clothes that might fit Katsuo.

As she sat at her sewing machine, Katsuo accumulated a wardrobe. She thought of making herself some fashionable new hats, but she had no time for that. At the machine, she forgot her sorrows. The hum and the mechanical movements cut off that other erratic melody, her emotional ups and downs.

Why had she not tried this mechanical cutting-off of the emotions earlier? But then of course it came at a time when her heart no longer put up the resistance it would once have. One day she pricked her finger, and a drop of blood oozed out. She was frightened. Pain was associated with death.

But the fear was followed by a different emotion: if such a trivial accident should indeed bring death, that would be an answer to a prayer. She spent more and more time at the machine. It was the safest of machines, however. It did not even touch her.

Even now, she was dissatisfied, waiting for something. Masaru would turn away from this vague seeking, and they would go for a whole day without speaking to each other.

Winter approached. The tomb was ready, and the ashes were buried.

In the loneliness of winter, one thinks longingly of summer.

Memories of summer threw an even sharper shadow across their lives. And yet the memories had come to seem like something out of a storybook. There was no avoiding the fact that, around the winter fire, everything took on an air of fiction.

In midwinter, there were signs that Tomoko was pregnant. For the first time, forgetfulness came as a natural right. Never before had they been quite so careful – it seemed strange that the child might be born safely, and only natural that they should lose it.

Everything was going well. A line was drawn between them and old memories. Borrowing strength from the child she was carrying, Tomoko for the first time had the courage to admit the pain was gone. She had only to recognize that fact.

Tomoko tried to understand. It is difficult to understand while an incident is before one's eyes, however. Understanding comes later. One analyses the emotions, and deduces, and explains to oneself. On looking back, Tomoko could not but feel dissatisfied with her inadequate emotions. There could be no doubt that the dissatisfaction would stay longer, a drag on her heart, than the sorrow itself. But there could be no going back for another try.

She refused to admit any incorrectness in her responses. She was a mother. And at the same time she could not leave off doubting.

While true forgetfulness had not yet come, something covered Tomoko's sorrow as a thin coating of ice covers a lake. Occasionally it would break, but overnight it would form again.

Forgetfulness began to show its real strength when they were not watching it. It filtered in. It found the tiniest opening, and filtered in. It attacked the organism like an invisible germ, it worked slowly but steadily. Tomoko was going through unconscious motions as when one resists a dream. She was most uneasy, resisting forgetfulness.

She told herself that forgetfulness came through the strength of the child inside her. But it was only helped by the child. The outlines of the incident were slowly giving way, dimming, blurring, weathering, disintegrating.

There had appeared in the summer sky a fearsome marble image, white and stark. It had dissolved into a cloud – the arms had dropped off, the head was gone, the long sword in the hand had fallen. The expression on the stone face had been enough to raise the hair, but slowly it had blurred and softened.

One day she switched off a radio drama about a mother who had lost a child. She was a little astonished at the promptness with which she thus disposed of the burden of memory. A mother awaiting her fourth child, she felt, had a moral obligation to resist the almost dissolute pleasure of losing herself in grief. Tomoko had changed in these last few months.

For the sake of the child, she must hold off dark waves of emotion. She must keep her inward balance. She was far more pleased with the dictates of mental hygiene than she could be with insidious forgetfulness. Above all, she felt free. With all the injunctions, she felt free. Forgetfulness was of course demonstrating its power. Tomoko was astonished at how easily managed her heart was.

She lost the habit of remembering, and it no longer seemed strange that the tears failed to come at memorial services or visits to the cemetery. She believed that she had become magnanimous, that she could forgive anything. When for instance spring came and she took Katsuo walking in a near-by park, she was no longer able to feel, even if she tried, the spite that would have swept over her immediately after the tragedy had she come upon children playing in the sand. Because she had forgiven them, all these children were living in peace. So it seemed to her.

While forgetfulness came to Masaru sooner than to his wife, that was no sign of coldness on his part. It was rather Masaru who had wallowed in sentimental grief. A man even in his fickleness is generally more sentimental than a woman. Unable to stretch out the emotion, and conscious of the fact that grief was not particularly stubborn in following him about, Masaru suddenly felt alone, and he allowed himself a trifling infidelity. He quickly tired of it. Tomoko became pregnant. He hurried back to her like a child hurrying to its mother.

The tragedy left them as a castaway leaves a sinking ship.

Soon they were able to view it as it must have seemed to people who noticed it in a corner of the newspapers that day. Tomoko and Masaru even wondered if they had had a part in it. Had they not been but the spectators who happened to be nearest? All who had actually participated in the incident had died, and would participate for ever. For us to have a part in a historical incident, our very existence must somehow be at stake. And what had Masaru and his wife had at stake? In the first place, had they had time to put anything at stake?

The incident shone far away, a lighthouse on a distant headland. It flashed on and off, like the revolving light on Cape Tsumeki, south of A. Beach. Rather than an injury it became a moral lesson, and it changed from a concrete fact to a metaphor. It was no longer the property of the Ikuta family, it was public. As the lighthouse shines on beach wastes, and on waves baring their white fangs at lonely rocks all through the night, and on the groves around it, so the incident shone on the complex everyday life around them. People should read the lesson. An old, simple lesson that parents may be expected to have engraved on their minds: You have to watch children constantly when you take them to the beach. People drown where you would never think it possible.

Not that Masaru and his wife had sacrificed two children and a sister to teach a lesson. The loss of the three had served no other purpose, however; and many a heroic death produces as little.

Tomoko's fourth child was a girl, born late in the summer. Their happiness was unbounded. Masaru's parents came from Kanazawa to see the new grandchild, and while they were in Tokyo Masaru took them to the cemetery.

They named the child Momoko. Mother and child did well – Tomoko knew how to take care of a baby. And Katsuo was delighted to have a sister again.

It was the following summer – two years after the drowning, a year after Momoko's birth. Tomoko startled Masaru by saying she wanted to go to A. Beach.

'Didn't you say you would never go there again?'

'But I want to.'

'Aren't you strange? I don't want to at all, myself.'

'Oh? Let's forget about it, then.'

She was silent for two or three days. Then she said: 'I *would* like to go.'

'Go by yourself.'

'I couldn't.'

'Why?'

'I'd be afraid.'

'Why do you want to go to a place you're afraid of?'

'I want all of us to go. We would have been all right if you'd been along. I want you to go too.'

'You can't tell what might happen if you stay too long. And I can't take much time off.'

'One night will be enough.'

'But it's such an out-of-the-way place.'

He asked her again what had made her want to go. She only answered that she did not know. Then he remembered one of the rules in the detective stories he was so fond of: the murderer always wants to go back to the scene of the crime, whatever the risks. Tomoko was taken by a strange impulse to revisit the place where the children died.

Tomoko asked a third time – with no particular urgency, in the same monotonous way as before – and Masaru determined to take two days off, avoiding the week-end crowds. The Eirakusō was the only inn at A. Beach. They reserved rooms as far as possible from that unhappy room. Tomoko as always refused to drive with her husband when the children were along. The four of them, husband and wife and Katsuo and Momoko, took a taxi from Itō.

It was the height of the summer. Behind the houses along the way were sunflowers, shaggy as lions' manes. The taxi scattered dust on the open, honest faces, but the sunflowers seemed quite undisturbed.

As the sea came in sight to the left, Katsuo gave a squeal of delight. He was five now, and it was two years since he had last been to the coast.

They talked little in the taxi. It was shaking too violently to be the best place for conversation. Momoko now and then said something they understood. Katsuo taught her the word 'sea', and she pointed out of the other window at the bald red mountain and said: 'Sea.' To Masaru it was as if Katsuo were teaching the baby an unlucky word.

They arrived at the Eirakusō, and the same manager came out. Masaru tipped him. He remembered only too clearly how his hand had trembled with that other thousand-yen note.

The inn was quiet. It was a bad year. Masaru began remembering things and became irritable. He scolded his wife in front of the children.

'Why the devil did we come here? We only remember things we don't want to. Things we had finally forgotten. There are any number of decent places we could have gone to on our first trip with Momoko. And I'm too busy to be taking foolish trips.'

'But you agreed to, didn't you?'

'You kept at me.'

The grass was baking in the afternoon sun. Everything was exactly as two years before. A blue-green-and-red swimming suit was drying on the white swing. Two or three quoits lay around the peg, half-hidden in the grass. The lawn was shady where Yasue's body had lain. The sun, leaking through the trees to the bare grass, stemmed suddenly to dapple the undulations of Yasue's green bathing suit – it was the way the flecks of light moved with the wind. Masaru did not know that the body had lain there. Only Tomoko had the illusion. Just as for Masaru the incident itself had not happened while he did not know of it, so that patch of grass would be for ever only a quiet, shady corner. For him, and still more for the other guests, thought Tomoko.

His wife was silent, and Masaru tired of scolding her. Katsuo went down into the garden and rolled a quoit across the grass. He squatted down and watched intently to see where it would go. It bounced awkwardly through the shadows, took a sudden jump, and fell. Katsuo watched, motionless. He thought it should get up again.

The cicadas were humming. Masaru, now silent, felt the sweat coming out around his collar. He remembered his duty as a father. 'Let's go down to the beach, Katsuo.'

Tomoko carried Momoko. The four of them went through the gate in the hedge and out under the pine-trees. The waves came in swiftly and spread shining over the beach.

It was low tide, and they could make their way round the rock to the beach. Taking Katsuo by the hand, Masaru walked across the hot sands in pattens borrowed from the inn.

There was not a single beach umbrella. They could see no more than twenty people the whole length of the bathing beach, which began from just beyond the rock.

They stood silently at the edge of the water.

There were grand clusters of clouds again today, piled one upon another. It seemed strange that a mass so heavy with light could be borne in the air. Above the packed clouds at the horizon, light clouds trailed away as though left behind in the blue by a broom. The clouds below seemed to be enduring something, holding out against something. Excesses of light and shade cloaked in form, a dark, inchoate passion shaped by a will radiant and architectural, as in music.

From beneath the clouds, the sea came towards them, far wider and more changeless than the land. The land never seems to take the sea, even its inlets. Particularly along a wide bow of coast, the sea sweeps in from everywhere.

The waves came up, broke, fell back. Their thunder was like the intense quiet of the summer sun, hardly a noise at all. Rather an ear-splitting silence. A lyrical transformation of the waves, not waves, but rather ripples one might call the light, derisive laughter of the waves at themselves – ripples came up to their feet, and retreated again.

Masaru glanced sideways at his wife.

She was gazing out to sea. Her hair blew in the sea breeze, and she seemed undismayed at the sun. Her eyes were moist and almost regal. Her mouth was closed tight. In her arms she held one-year-old Mokomo, who wore a little straw hat.

Masaru had seen that face before. Since the tragedy, Tomoko's face had often worn that expression, as if she had forgotten herself, and as if she were waiting for something.

'What are you waiting for?' he wanted to ask lightly.

But the words did not come. He thought he knew without asking.

He clutched tighter at Katsuo's hand.

Translated and abridged by Edward G. Seidensticker

Three Million Yen

'We're to meet her at nine?' asked Kenzō.

'At nine, she said, in the toy department on the ground floor,' replied Kiyoko. 'But it's too noisy to talk there, and I told her about the coffee shop on the third floor instead.'

'That was a good idea.'

The young husband and wife looked up at the neon pagoda atop the New World Building, which they were approaching from the rear.

It was a cloudy, muggy night, of a sort common in the early-summer rainy season. Neon lights painted the low sky in rich colours. The delicate pagoda, flashing on and off in the softer of neon tones, was very beautiful indeed. It was particularly beautiful when, after all the flashing neon tubes had gone out together, they suddenly flashed on again, so soon that the after-image had scarcely disappeared. To be seen from all over Asakusa, the pagoda had replaced Gourd Pond, now filled in, as the main landmark of the Asakusa night.

To Kenzō and Kiyoko the pagoda seemed to encompass in all its purity some grand, inaccessible dream of life. Leaning against the rail of the parking lot, they looked absently up at it for a time.

Kenzō was in an undershirt, cheap trousers, and wooden clogs. His skin was fair but the lines of the shoulders and chest were powerful, and bushes of black hair showed between the mounds of muscle at the armpits. Kiyoko, in a sleeveless dress, always had her own armpits carefully shaved. Kenzō was very fussy. Because they hurt when the hair began to grow again, she had become almost obsessive about keeping them shaved, and there was a faint flush on the white skin.

She had a round little face, the pretty features as though

woven of cloth. It reminded one of some earnest, unsmiling little animal. It was a face which a person trusted immediately, but not one on which to read thoughts. On her arm she had a large pink plastic handbag and Kenzō's pale blue sports shirt. Kenzō liked to be empty-handed.

From her modest coiffure and make-up one sensed the frugality of their life. Her eyes were clear and had no time for other men.

They crossed the dark road in front of the parking lot and went into the New World. The big market on the ground floor was filled with myriad-coloured mountains of splendid, gleaming, cheap wares, and salesgirls peeped from crevices in the mountains. Cool fluorescent lighting poured over the scene. Behind a grove of antimony models of the Tokyo Tower was a row of mirrors painted with Tokyo scenes, and in them, as the two passed, were rippling, waving images of the mountain of ties and summer shirts opposite.

'I couldn't stand living in a place with so many mirrors,' said Kiyoko. 'I'd be embarrassed.'

'Nothing to be embarrassed about.' Though his manner was gruff, Kenzō was not one to ignore what his wife said, and his answers were generally perceptive. The two had come to the toy department.

'She knows how you love the toy department. That's why she said to meet her here.'

Kenzō laughed. He was fond of the trains and automobiles and space missiles, and he always embarrassed Kiyoko, getting an explanation for each one and trying each one out, but never buying. She took his arm and steered him some distance from the counter.

'It's easy to see that you want a boy. Look at the toys you pick.'

'I don't care whether it's a boy or a girl. I just wish it would come soon.'

'Another two years, that's all.'

'Everything according to plan.'

They had divided the savings account they were so assiduously building up into several parts, labelled Plan X and Plan Y and Plan Z and the like. Children must come strictly according to plan. However much they might want a child now, it would have to wait until sufficient money for Plan X had accumulated. Seeing the inadvisability, for numerous reasons, of hire-purchase, they waited until the money for Plan A or Plan B or Plan C had accumulated, and then paid cash for an electric washing machine or refrigerator or a television set. Plan A and Plan B had already been carried out. Plan D required little money, but since it had as its object a low-priority wardrobe, it was always being pushed back. Neither of them was much interested in clothes. What they had they could hang in the cloak-room, and all they really needed was enough to keep them warm in the winter.

They were very cautious when making a large purchase. They collected catalogues and looked at various possibilities and asked the advice of people who had already made the purchase, and, when the time for buying finally came, went off to a wholesaler in Okachimachi.

A child was still more serious. First there had to be a secure livelihood and enough money, more than enough money, to see that the child had surroundings of which a parent need not be ashamed, if not, perhaps, enough to see it all the way to adulthood. Kenzō had already made thorough inquiries with friends who had children, and knew what expenditures for powdered milk could be considered reasonable.

With their own plans so nicely formed, the two had nothing but contempt for the thoughtless, floundering ways of the poor. Children were to be produced according to plan in surroundings ideal for rearing them, and the best days were waiting after a child had arrived. Yet they were sensible enough not to pursue their dreams too far. They kept their eyes on the light immediately before them.

There was nothing that enraged Kenzō more than the view of the young that life in contemporary Japan was without hope. He was not a person given to deep thinking, but he had an almost religious faith that if a man respected nature and was obedient to it, and if he but made an effort for himself, the way would somehow open. The first thing was reverence for nature, founded on connubial affection. The greatest antidote for despair was the faith of a man and woman in each other.

Fortunately, he was in love with Kiyoko. To face the future hopefully, therefore, he had only to follow the conditions laid down by nature. Now and then some other woman made a motion in his direction, but he sensed something unnatural in pleasure for the sake of pleasure. It was better to listen to Kiyoko complaining about the dreadful price these days of vegetables and fish.

The two had made a round of the market and were back at the toy department.

Kenzō's eyes were riveted to the toy before him, a station for flying saucers. On the sheet-metal base the complicated mechanism was painted as if viewed through a window, and a revolving light flashed on and off inside the control tower. The flying saucer, of deep blue plastic, worked on the old principle of the flying top. The station was apparently suspended in space, for the background of the metal base was covered with stars and clouds, among the former the familiar rings of Saturn.

The bright stars of the summer night were splendid. The painted metal surface was indescribably cool, and it was as if all the discomfort of the muggy night would go if a person but gave himself up to that sky.

Before Kiyoko could stop him, Kenzō had resolutely snapped a spring at one corner of the station.

The saucer went spinning towards the ceiling.

The salesgirl reached out and gave a little cry.

The saucer described a gentle arc towards the pastry counter across the aisle and settled square on the million-yen biscuits.

'We're in!' Kenzō ran over to it.

'What do you mean, we're in?' Embarrassed, Kiyoko turned quickly away from the salesgirl and started after him.

'Look. Look where it landed. This means good luck. Not a doubt about it.'

The oblong biscuits were in the shape of decidedly large banknotes, and the baked-in design, again like a banknote, carried the words 'One Million Yen'. On the printed label of the cellophane wrapper, the figure of a bald shopkeeper took the place of Prince Shōtoku, who decorates most banknotes. There were three large biscuits in each package.

Over the objections of Kiyoko, who thought fifty yen for these biscuits ridiculous, Kenzō bought a package to make doubly sure of the good luck. He immediately broke the wrapping, gave a biscuit to Kiyoko, and took one himself. The third went into her handbag.

As his strong teeth bit into the biscuit, a sweet, slightly bitter taste flowed into his mouth. Kiyoko took a little mouselike bite from her own biscuit, almost too large for her grasp.

Kenzō brought the flying saucer back to the toy counter. The salesgirl, out of sorts, looked away as she reached to take it.

Kiyoko had high, arched breasts, and, though she was small, her figure was good. When she walked with Kenzō she seemed to be hiding in his shadow. At street crossings he would take her arm firmly, look to the right and the left, and help her across, pleased at the feel of the rich flesh.

Kenzō liked the pliant strength in a woman who, although she could perfectly well do things for herself, always deferred to her husband. Kiyoko had never read a newspaper, but she had an astonishingly accurate knowledge of her surroundings. When she took a comb in her hand or turned over the leaf of a calendar or folded a summer kimono, it was not as if she were engaged in housework, but rather as if, fresh and alert, she were keeping company with the 'things' known as comb and calendar and kimono. She soaked in her world of things as she might soak in a bath.

'There's an indoor amusement park on the fourth floor. We can kill time there,' said Kenzō. Kiyoko followed silently into a waiting lift, but when they reached the fourth floor she tugged at his belt.

'It's a waste of money. Everything seems so cheap, but it's all arranged so that you spend more money than you intend to.'

'That's no way to talk. This is our good night, and if you tell yourself it's like a first-run movie it doesn't seem so expensive.'

'What's the sense in a first-run movie? If you wait a little while you can see it for half as much.'

Her earnestness was most engaging. A brown smudge from the biscuit clung to her puckered lips.

'Wipe your mouth,' said Kenzō. 'You're making a mess of yourself.'

Kiyoko looked into a mirror on a near-by pillar and removed the smear with the nail of her little finger. She still had two-thirds of a biscuit in her hand.

They were at the entrance to 'Twenty Thousand Leagues Under the Sea'. Jagged rocks reached to the ceiling, and the porthole of a submarine on the sea floor served as the ticket window: forty yen for adults, twenty yen for children.

'But forty yen is too high,' said Kiyoko, turning away from the mirror. 'You aren't any less hungry after you look at all those cardboard fish, and for forty yen you can get a hundred grams of the best kind of real fish.'

'Yesterday they wanted forty for a cut of black snapper. Oh, well. When you're chewing on a million yen you don't talk like a beggar.'

The brief debate finished, Kenzō bought the tickets.

'You've let that biscuit go to your head.'

'But it isn't bad at all. Just right when you're hungry.'

'You just ate.'

At a landing like a railway platform five or six little boxcars, each large enough for two people, stood at intervals along a track. Three or four other couples were waiting, but the two climbed unabashedly into a car. It was in fact a little tight for two, and Kenzō had to put his arm around his wife's shoulders.

The operator was whistling somewhat disdainfully. Kenzō's powerful arm, on which the sweat had dried, was solid against Kiyoko's naked shoulders and back. Naked skin clung to naked skin like the layers of some intricately folded insect's wing. The car began to shake.

'I'm afraid,' said Kiyoko, with the expression of one not in the least afraid.

The cars, each some distance from the rest, plunged into a

dark tunnel of rock. Immediately inside there was a sharp curve, and the reverberations were deafening.

A huge shark with shining green scales passed, almost brushing their heads, and Kiyoko ducked away. As she clung to her young husband he gave her a kiss. After the shark had passed, the car ground round a curve in pitch darkness again, but his lips landed unerringly on hers, little fish speared in the dark. The little fish jumped and were still.

The darkness made Kiyoko strangely shy. Only the violent shaking and grinding sustained her. As she slipped deep into the tunnel, her husband's arms around her, she felt naked and flushed crimson. The darkness, dense and impenetrable, had a strength that seemed to render clothes useless. She thought of a dark shed she had secretly played in as a child.

Like a flower springing from the darkness, a red beam of light flashed at them, and Kiyoko cried out once more. It was the wide, gaping mouth of a big angler fish on the ocean floor. Around it, coral fought with the poisonous dark green of seaweed.

Kenzō put his cheek to his wife's – she was still clinging to him – and with the fingers of the arm around her shoulders played with her hair. Compared to the motion of the car the motion of the fingers was slow and deliberate. She knew that he was enjoying the show and enjoying her fright at it as well.

'Will it be over soon? I'm afraid.' But her voice was drowned out in the roar.

Once again they were in darkness. Though frightened, Kiyoko had her store of courage. Kenzō's arms were around her, and there was no fright and no shame she could not bear. Because hope had never left them, the state of happiness was for the two of them just such a state of tension.

A big, muddy octopus appeared before them. Once again Kiyoko cried out. Kenzō promptly kissed the nape of her neck. The great tentacles of the octopus filled the cave, and a fierce lightning darted from its eyes.

At the next curve a drowned corpse was standing disconsolately in a seaweed forest.

Finally the light at the far end began to show, the car slowed down, and they were liberated from the unpleasant noise. At the bright platform the uniformed attendant waited to catch the forward handle of the car.

'Is that all?' asked Kenzō.

The man said that it was.

Arching her back, Kiyoko climbed to the platform and whispered in Kenzō's ear: 'It makes you feel like a fool, paying forty yen for that.'

At the door they compared their biscuits. Kiyoko had two-thirds left, and Kenzō more than half.

'Just as big as when we came in,' said Kenzō. 'It was so full of thrills that we didn't have time to eat.'

'If you think about it that way, it doesn't seem so bad after all.'

Kenzō's eyes were already on the gaudy sign by another door. Electric decorations danced around the word 'Magicland', and green and red lights flashed on and off in the startled eyes of a cluster of dwarfs, their domino costumes shining in gold and silver dust. A bit shy about suggesting immediately that they go in, Kenzō leaned against the wall and munched away at his biscuit.

'Remember how we crossed the parking lot? The light brought out our shadows on the ground, maybe two feet apart, and a funny idea came to me. I thought to myself how it would be if a little boy's shadow bobbed up and we took it by the hand. And just then a shadow really did break away from ours and come between them.'

'No!'

'Then I looked round, and it was someone behind us. A couple of drivers were playing catch, and one of them had dropped the ball and run after it.'

'One of these days we really will be out walking, three of us.'

'And we'll bring it here.' Kenzō motioned towards the sign. 'And so we ought to go in and have a look at it first.'

Kiyoko said nothing this time as he started for the ticket window.

Possibly because it was a bad time of the day, Magicland was not popular. On both sides of the path as they entered there were flashing banks of artificial flowers. A music box was playing.

'When we build our house this is the way we'll have the path.'

'But it's in very bad taste,' objected Kiyoko.

How would it feel to go into a house of your own? A building fund had not yet appeared in the plans of the two, but in due course it would. Things they scarcely dreamed of would one day appear in the most natural way imaginable. Usually so prudent, they let their dreams run on this evening, perhaps, as Kiyoko said, because the million-yen biscuits had gone to their heads.

Great artificial butterflies were taking honey from the artificial flowers. Some were as big as brief-cases, and there were yellow and black spots on their translucent red wings. Tiny bulbs flashed on and off in their protuberant eyes. In the light from below, a soft aura as of sunset in a mist bathed the plastic flowers and grasses. It may have been dust rising from the floor.

The first room they came to, following the arrow, was the leaning room. The floor and all the furnishings leaned so that when one entered upright there was a grating, discordant note to the room.

'Not the sort of house I'd want to live in,' said Kenzō, bracing himself against a table on which there were yellow wooden tulips. The words were like a command. He was not himself aware of it, but his decisiveness was that of the privileged one whose hope and well-being refuse to admit outsiders. It was not strange that in the hope there was a scorn for the hopes of others and that no one was allowed to lay a finger on the well-being.

Braced against the leaning table, the determined figure in the undershirt made Kiyoko smile. It was a very domestic scene. Kenzō was like an outraged young man who, having built an extra room on his Sundays, had made a mistake somewhere and ended up with the windows and floors all askew.

'You *could* live in a place like this, though,' said Kiyoko.

Spreading her arms like a mechanical doll, she leaned forward as the room leaned, and her face approached Kenzō's broad left shoulder at the same angle as the wooden tulips.

His brow wrinkled in a serious young frown, Kenzō smiled. He kissed the cheek that leaned towards him and bit roughly into his million-yen biscuit.

By the time they had emerged from the wobbly staircases, the shaking passageways, the log bridges from the railings of which monster heads protruded, and numerous other curious places as well, the heat was too much for them. Kenzō finished his own biscuit, took what was left of his wife's between his teeth, and set out in search of a cool evening breeze. Beyond a row of rocking-horses, a door led out to a balcony.

'What time is it?' asked Kiyoko.

'A quarter to nine. Let's go out and cool off till nine.'

'I'm thirsty. The biscuit was so dry.' She fanned at her perspiring white throat with Kenzō's sports shirt.

'In a minute you can have something to drink.'

The night breeze was cool on the wide balcony. Kenzō yawned a wide yawn and leaned against the railing beside his wife. Bare young arms caressed the black railing, wet with the night dew.

'It's much cooler than when we came in.'

'Don't be silly,' said Kenzō. 'It's just higher.'

Far below, the black machines of the outdoor amusement park seemed to slumber. The bare seats of the merry-go-round, slightly inclined, were exposed to the dew. Between the iron bars of the aerial observation car, suspended chairs swayed gently in the breeze.

The liveliness of the restaurant to the left was in complete contrast. They had a bird's-eye view into all the corners of the wide expanse inside its walls. Everything was there to look at, as if on a stage: the roofs of the separate cottages, the passages joining them, the ponds and brooks in the garden, the stone lanterns, the interiors of the Japanese rooms, some with serving maids whose kimono sleeves were held up by red cords, others with dancing geisha. The strings of lanterns at the eaves were beautiful, and their white lettering was beautiful too.

The wind carried away the noises of the place, and there was something almost mystically beautiful about it, congealed in delicate detail there at the bottom of the murky summer night.

'I'll bet it's expensive.' Kiyoko was once more at her favourite romantic topic.

'Naturally. Only a fool would go there.'

'I'll bet they say that cucumbers are a great delicacy, and they charge some fantastic price. How much?'

'Two hundred, maybe.' Kenzō took his sports shirt and started to put it on.

Buttoning it for him, Kiyoko continued: 'They must think their customers are fools. Why, that's ten times what cucumbers are worth. You can get three of the very best for twenty yen.'

'Oh? They're getting cheap.'

'The price started going down a week or so ago.'

It was five to nine. They went out to look for a stairway to the coffee shop on the third floor. Two of the biscuits had disappeared. The other was too large for Kiyoko's very large handbag, and protruded from the unfastened clasp.

The old lady, an impatient person, had arrived early and was waiting. The seats from which the loud jazz orchestra could best be seen were all taken, but there were vacant places where the bandstand was out of sight, beside the potted palm probably rented from some gardener. Sitting alone in a summer kimono, the old lady seemed wholly out of place.

She was a small woman not far past middle age, and she had the clean, well-tended face of the plebeian lowlands. She spoke briskly with many delicate gestures. She was proud of the fact that she got on so nicely with young people.

'You'll be treating me, of course, so I ordered something expensive while I was waiting.' Even as she spoke the tall glass arrived, pieces of fruit atop a parfait.

'Now that was generous of you. All we needed was soda water.'

Her outstretched little finger taut, the old lady plunged in with her spoon and skilfully brought out the cream beneath. Meanwhile she was talking along at her usual brisk pace.

'It's nice that this place is so noisy and no one can hear us. Tonight we go to Nakano – I think I mentioned it over the phone. An ordinary private house and – can you imagine it? – the customers are housewives having a class reunion. There's not much that the rich ladies don't know about these days. And I imagine they walk around pretending the idea never entered their heads. Anyway, I told them about you, and they said they had to have you and no one else. They don't want someone who's all beaten up by the years, you know. And I must say that I can't blame them. So I asked a good stiff price and she said it was low and if they were pleased they'd give you a good tip. They haven't any idea what the market rate is, of course. But I want you to do your best, now. I'm sure I don't need to tell you, but if they're pleased we'll get all sorts of rich customers. There aren't many that go as well together as you two do, of course, and I'm not worried, but don't do anything to make me ashamed of you. Well, anyhow, the woman of the house is the wife of some important person or other, and she'll be waiting for us at the coffee shop in front of Nakano station. You know what will happen next. She'll send the taxi through all sorts of back alleys to get us mixed up. I don't imagine she'll blindfold us, but she'll pull us through the back door so we don't have a chance to read the sign on the gate. I won't like it any better than you will, but she has herself to consider, after all. Don't let it bother you. Me? Oh, I'll be doing the usual thing, keeping watch in the hall. I can bluff my way through, I don't care who comes in. Well, maybe we ought to get started. And let me say it again, I want a good performance from you.'

It was late in the night, and Kiyoko and Kenzō had left the old lady and were back in Asakusa. They were even more exhausted than usual. Kenzō's wooden clogs dragged along the street. The billboards in the park were a poisonous black under the cloudy sky.

Simultaneously, they looked up at the New World. The neon pagoda was dark.

'What a rotten bunch. I don't thing I've ever seen such a rotten, stuck-up bunch,' said Kenzō.

Her eyes on the ground, Kiyoko did not answer.

'Well? Did you ever see a worse bunch of affected old women?'

'No. But what can you do? The pay was good.'

'Playing around with money they pry from their husbands. Don't get to be that way when you have money.'

'Silly.' Kiyoko's smiling face was sharply white in the darkness.

'A really nasty bunch.' Kenzō spat in a strong white arc. 'How much?'

'This.' Kiyoko reached artlessly into her handbag and pulled out some notes.

'Five thousand? We've never made that much before. And the old woman took three thousand. Damn! I'd like to tear it up, that's what I'd like to do. That would really feel good.'

Kiyoko took the money back in some consternation. Her finger touched the last of the million-yen biscuits.

'Tear this up in its place,' she said softly.

Kenzō took the biscuit, wadded the cellophane wrapper, and threw it to the ground. It crackled sharply on the silent, deserted street. Too large for one hand, he took the biscuit in both hands and tried to break it. It was damp and soggy, and the sweet surface stuck to his hands. The more it bent the more it resisted. He was in the end unable to break it.

Translated by Edward G. Seidensticker

Thermos Flasks

Kawase, who had been in Los Angeles for six months on company business, could have gone directly back to Japan, but was staying in San Francisco for a few days. Looking over the San Francisco *Chronicle* in his hotel, he suddenly wanted to read something in Japanese and took out a letter that had come to Los Angeles from his wife.

'Shigeru seems to remember his father from time to time. For no reason at all, he will get a worried expression and say: "Where's papa?" The thermos flask still works very well when he is bad. Your sister from Setagaya was here the other day and said that she had never heard of a child who was afraid of thermos flasks. Maybe because it's old, the thermos flask leaks air round the cork, even when you put it down very gently, and makes noises like some old man complaining to himself. Shigeru always decides to behave when he hears it. I'm sure he is more afraid of the thermos flask than of his indulgent father.'

When he had finished rereading the letter, by now almost memorized, Kawase had nothing else to do. It was a bright October day, but all the lights were on in the lobby, which was most depressing. Old people, dressed in their best despite the earliness of the hour, made limp motions like waving seaweed. The monocle of one old man caught the light as he read his newspaper in a deep armchair.

Weaving through the many-coloured luggage of what appeared to be a party of tourists, Kawase left his key at the desk – it was busy as always – and pushed open the heavy glass door.

He crossed Geary Street in the blinding autumn sunlight and turned down Powell Street, with its coffee shops and gift shops and cheap night clubs, and a sea-food restaurant that had the prow of a clipper at the door. From far away he picked out a figure coming towards him.

Despite the distance, he knew immediately that it was a Japanese woman, not second or third generation, but native Japanese. It was not that she wore Japanese dress. Carefully imitating the conservative dress of the city, she had on a hat, a pearl necklace, and a good silver-mink coat. Yet her powdered face was a trifle too white, and though there were no obvious flaws in her dress, her determined walk had something unnatural about it. As a result the child whose hand she held was half-dangling in the air.

'Well!' The exclamation was so loud that people turned to look, and the pointed toes of the high-heeled shoes darted at him in tiny steps. 'I recognized you right away. You can always tell a Japanese, even from the distance. You walk as if you ought to have a pair of swords in your belt.'

'And what do you think you look like?' Kawase too forgot the greetings one exchanges with an acquaintance not seen for a very long time. It was as if the distance between past and present, usually so precise, had shrunk a few inches.

He blamed the shrinkage on the foreign country. The Japanese system of measuring had gone askew. There were times when a sudden encounter abroad produced effusions that were cause for later regret, for the distance could not be forced back to normal afterwards. The difficulty was not limited to relations between men and women. Kawase had had the experience with other men, and men who were not particularly close friends.

It was more than evident that the woman had undergone rigorous training this last year or two in how to wear Western clothes and Western cosmetics. The results were considerable, but the uneasiness of the new arrival showed in the way she applied face powder. Western women think nothing of opening their compacts in public and scattering powder about, and yet there is a certain casualness in the results, with bare spots left showing beside the nose. There was nothing casual about this woman's make-up.

As they stood talking, they first explained what had brought them here.

The exporter who was her patron came frequently to the United States, and he had sent her on an inspection trip preparatory to opening a new sort of Japanese restaurant in San Francisco. She would probably become the manager, but it was not as if her patron were exiling an unwanted mistress. Rather she felt as she might if he were to open an inn for her in Atami or some other resort near Tokyo. He was an entrepreneur on the heroic scale.

The child was growing impatient.

'Let's have a cup of tea.' The woman spoke quite as if they were walking down the Ginza together. Kawase agreed, since he had nothing else to do, but he did not know what to call her. Asaka or Faint Perfume, her professional name as a geisha some five years before, would scarcely do.

2

The coffee shop was not of the elaborate sort they might have found on the Ginza. A noisy dining-room for short orders, a long counter winding around the centre, a noisy shop selling tobacco and gifts, and nothing more. Kawase lifted the little girl to a stool at the counter. It was the natural arrangement to put her between them and talk over her head. She was a silent child, and her weight and warmth left a sort of faint, pleasant recollection in the muscles of Kawase's arms.

There were no other Orientals in the place. The stainless steel round the service window clouded with steam and quickly cleared again, reflecting the white aprons of the waitresses. They were all middle-aged women heavily made up. Though they exchanged brief greetings with regular customers they were not quick to smile.

'Clark Gable's wife is in San Francisco,' said the blonde woman on Kawase's left. 'I met her at a party.'

'Oh? She must be getting along in years.'

Turning half an ear on the conversation, Asaka took off her coat and bundled it around her hips. Only at the nape of the neck, which she no longer needed to worry about as she had as a geisha, did she show the easy negligence of the professional woman turned amateur again. She wore her hair up, and Kawase was startled at how dark the skin was.

'They aren't very friendly but they do work hard,' said Asaka in a loud voice, motioning to the waitresses with her eyes. Kawase was pleased to see in the roving eyes how enthusiasm for her new work took in everything around her. She had always been beautiful, he thought, when he had been able to look at her as if he were watching a distant fire.

Delighted at being able to speak Japanese, Asaka chattered on about the preparations for her trip to the United States. First she had learned English from her patron. She had quite given up Japanese music, both old and popular, and devoted all of her spare time to linguaphone records. She had adopted Western clothes, which she had earlier worn only in the worst of the summer heat, and she had made daily trips to an expensive seamstress. She had asked her patron for advice and instruction on all the colours and designs. It appeared that the patron was not a man to make a clear distinction between lechery and education, and he could not have had better material than Asaka for building a woman to his taste. She may have danced the mambo in kimono in night clubs, but never before, it would seem, had a man so assiduously instructed her in 'the West'. And never before had a man found a woman who responded more favourably.

Their orders came as she was finishing the long story. With a stiff, perfunctory smile, the waitress slammed a vanilla milk shake before the wide-eyed little girl. The glass must have held all of a pint.

'My name is Hamako,' said Asaka, rather belatedly introducing her daughter. 'How do you do.' She put her hand to the child's head and urged her to bow. Hamako declined to do so, however. Instead she knelt on the stool and concentrated on the straw. She was too small to reach it sitting down.

It pleased Kawase that the child was not one for ceremony. Her features were good, resembling those of her mother, and her profile, as she sucked at the straw and brushed away hair with her outspread hand, was very pretty. She was quiet, leaving conversation to her elders.

'People are always asking how I could have produced such a quiet child.' But immediately Aska returned to more adult topics.

The shop was filled with a peculiarly American odour, half the hygienic smell of medicines, half the sweet, clinging odour of bodies. The customers were almost all women, middle-aged or older, with proud eyes and heavily painted lips, attacking large sweets and open sandwiches. Despite the noise and bustle of the store, there was something very lonely about the individual ..omen and their appetites. Sad, lonely, like a performance by so many consuming machines.

'I want a ride on the cable car,' said Hamako, who had half emptied her glass.

'That's what she wants every day. And we can perfectly well afford a taxi.'

'Oh, the richest tourists ride on the cable car. You won't be lowering yourself.'

'Is that sarcasm? But I'm not surprised. You were something of a needler in the old days.'

It was Asaka's first mention of 'the old days'.

'Well, I'll take you for a ride on the cable car if your mother won't.' Kawase slipped a quarter under the saucer and picked up the bill. He shook his head. He did not have a headache, but now that he was on the way home, all the weariness of travel seemed to collect in one place. He thought that a cable-car ride might clear it away.

Preparatory to helping Hamako down, Asaka squirmed back into her mink coat. Kawase helped her.

'I'm always forgetting. The gentleman is supposed to help. I'm not used to such kindness.'

'You'll have to learn to be more arrogant.'

'To be more dignified.'

Asaka sat up on the stool and arched her back. The young swelling of her suit coat was such as to arouse the envy of the women around the counter. Kawase remembered how in the old days he would stand behind her as she arched her back just so, and help tie her obi. Compared to the stiff, clean austerity of the obi, the softness of the mink coat seemed to evade the grasp.

A strange simile came into Kawase's mind: it was as if the great, vermilion-lacquered, black-riveted gate of some noble lady's mansion were suddenly to change into a slick revolving door.

3

They avoided talk of the old days, like a pair weaving in and out among puddles after a rainstorm, so deftly that neither of them found the process awkward. For talk of the present, they had only San Francisco. They were two travellers who had no other life.

The more he looked at her the more he could see behind her Western elegance the influence of that educator, her patron. The Asaka of old was something of an expert on the Japanese dance, and she would naturally fall into dance poses, her delicate fingers in a formal pattern, when she brought her hand to her mouth to laugh or was frightened or heard something she would rather not have heard. Now everything was changed. Yet she had not really acquired Western elegance in place of the old Japanese elegance. Her movements were remarkably angular. Kawase could imagine how unceasing had been her patron's labours in correcting all those little mannerisms. It was as if he had sent her off to America with his fingerprints on every part of her body. Only the too-white powder remained as a relic of the old days. Perhaps that was her one gesture of defiance, alone in a foreign country. As a matter of fact, however, it had once been much whiter.

As Asaka stood waiting for the cable car, the child's hand in hers, Kawase looked afresh at the mink coat and wondered where she would be keeping her little packet of paper handkerchiefs. In the old days she had always had a supply in her obi. The paper made itself felt in many delicate ways when they spent the night together. Kawase was in the habit of dancing with his hand on the bow of the obi, and he would come on the warm swelling of the paper, and deliberately rustle it as they danced. A smile, intimate and wary of being seen, would come to her lips. Sometimes, seated languidly with her legs curled beneath her, she would start to untie her obi, and there would be a soft gesture as she first took out the paper and laid it on the *tatami* matting. A certain heaviness in the motion told of the dampness of late night in the rainy season. On such a night, Kawase would slip his hand into the bow of the obi, and it would be as warm and moist as the inside of a tight closet. He could scarcely imagine that when, later, the obi was untied it would give forth that clean, cool, silken sound. And then, as the first morning light came through the frosted-glass window of the inn, the paper on the floor would light up, and he would watch daybreak from the white square. Asaka never forgot to take out the paper when she undid her obi, but sometimes she would forget to put it back when they dressed the following morning. And sometimes when they were quarrelling, the paper would be there, a clear, white sign on the matting. As these memories passed through his mind, Kawase concluded that nowhere on the mink-coated figure was there room for that swelling packet. A little white window had been painted over.

The cable car came and the three got on. With a nostalgic clang of its bell and a noise like a chest of drawers – such, too, the old streetcars of Tokyo had been – the cable car began to push its way industriously up Powell Street.

The rear half of the car was an ordinary closed trolley, but the front half had an open roof with benches, pillars, and standing-room on both sides of the motorman, who was grandly manipulating two long iron handles.

The old-fashioned car delighted Hamako. The three sat on one of the benches and watched windows slide down the hill before them. 'Isn't it fun,' said Hamako time after time. 'Isn't it fun.'

'Isn't it,' said Asaka, half to Kawase. It was as if the remark were to conceal the pleasure she felt herself. He sensed in the exchange her comradely way of making it appear that they were no ordinary, respectable mother and child.

At the top of the hill they got off the car and, since they had no business there, took another car down. The steep descent was even more interesting. Five or six middle-aged women, apparently tourists, shrieked and squealed as if they were in an amusement park, and looked round at the cool faces of native San Franciscans, seeking the reaction to their coquettishness. They were large women with faint moustaches, in coats of red and green.

Back at the square from which they had started, Asaka politely took her leave. She had an appointment for lunch, she said, but would like to have dinner with Kawase if he was free. Kawase took Hamako's hand and walked with them to his hotel, which was very near the square.

They stopped before a show window full of picnic things. The picnic set, all in Scotch plaid, was quite blinding, but the contrast with the artificial grass was very pleasant. The arrangement was done with careful casualness. It could have been left scattered by picnickers who had gone down to the river to wash their hands, and whose bright laughter came back up from the river.

'You'd never find a set like this in Japan,' said Asaka, her nose almost against the glass. It occurred to Kawase that she had probably gone through childhood with no knowledge of picnics. Sometimes she showed an intense longing for childish things. Once he had been unable to pry her from a window full of festival dolls. Either her patron, so intent on educating her in the Western way, had not noticed this side of her nature, or he was ignoring it. Kawase felt confident in his own perceptiveness.

Lost in the display, Asaka seemed to forget his presence. Suddenly she pointed at a thermos flask covered with Scotch plaid.

'Hamako. You're a big girl now, and you aren't afraid of that any more, are you?'

'No.'

'But you still remember the days when you were?'

'No.'

'There she is, answering just like a grown-up.' Asaka smiled as if, for the first time, to seek Kawase's assent. Kawase had been looking at the bright sunlight on the pavement, and the smiling face turned towards him seemed to mix with the brilliant white after-image like some weird, luminous mask floating in the air. He had only been half listening to the exchange, but he felt a painful knot in his chest. A moment later he saw that he must pretend not to understand a conversation that an outsider would not understand.

'What are you talking about?' he asked, trying to make the matter seem trivial.

'Nothing, really. But from the time she was about a year and a half old she was terrified of thermos flasks. If there's tea inside, it makes a funny bubbling noise round the cork, and she was terrified of that noise. When she wouldn't obey, I'd bring a thermos flask and threaten her with it. Not that I have to any more.'

'Children pick strange things to be afraid of.'

Asaka went on quite as if she were describing the child's unusual talents. 'But who ever heard of a child that was afraid of thermos flasks? Her grandmother had a good laugh over it. She said that Hamako would probably have a stroke if she grew up and the president of some thermos-flask company proposed to her.'

4

Asaka came by herself that evening. She had hired a Negro baby sitter at the hotel, and Hamako had taken remarkably well to the girl.

They had raw oysters and a crab sauté at a French restaurant called the Old Poodle Dog and finished in a blaze of cherries jubilee.

Kawase had recovered from the jolt the thermos flask had given him. He told himself that he was a victim of silly illusions and blamed his altogether too lively imagination.

The sadness of his wife's letter came back to him, and for no reason at all he felt that his own wife and child were far sadder than Asaka and her child. It was a foolish, baseless notion, and yet he could not put it from his mind.

Borrowing the strength of alcohol, he tried to flee from the present by turning to the forbidden subject of the old days.

'Was it during the rainy season, I wonder – once at a hotel you had stomach cramps and we had to call a doctor. You had us all in a cold sweat.'

'I thought I was going to die. And that brassy doctor only made things worse. I didn't like him at all.'

'The bill was high too.'

'I remember the kimono I had on that night. It was a summer kimono, naturally, heavy silk with horizontal stripes sewn so that stripes met at the seams in different colours. First a stripe of blurry sepia, maybe three inches wide, then a stripe of grey the same width, and on top of that white. Do you remember?'

'Very well.' In fact, the memory had dimmed.

'The obi was a good one too – two sprays of white bamboo on a vermilion background. But I never wore it again. I was always afraid of stomach cramps.'

It was a strange combination: a woman in a black cocktail suit, a jewelled pin on her breast, bringing a lipstick-smeared wineglass to her mouth time after time and talking of an old kimono.

Only a little more and Kawase would have said it: 'That business about the thermos flask this morning – it made me wonder if you were getting even with me after all these years. As a matter of fact, my own boy . . .' But he caught himself and closed his mouth just in time.

They had parted five years before in most unpleasant circumstances. The quarrel began when one of Asaka's colleagues, Kikuchiyo, passed on a secret to Kawase. She asked if Kawase knew that Asaka had been very friendly with a big export trader for some months, that he was going to redeem her from her obligations as a geisha, and that the two had already gone off together to Hakone a number of times. To Kawase this was startling news. Although it was broad daylight, he summoned Asaka to their usual rendezvous, a snack bar over a Ginza shoe-shop.

His indignation did not entirely make sense. One could ask, in the first place, if it was not out of proportion to his affection for her. All his relations with women contained a tacit understanding that he would not marry. He lost no opportunity to comment cynically on those who longed for normal married life, and he always demanded that the woman join in the laughter.

It followed that she would hold herself back in self-defence, and so the two would come to look upon their relationship as frank and sprightly. They wished and strove to think it so. Half for reasons of expediency and half for reasons of taste, Kawase was determined to have just such an affair with Asaka. In the end the effort touched their vanity and brought a dim light of despair, and an emptiness came into their quips and jokes. They fell into the illusion that they were beyond being wounded.

Then Kikuchiyo brought her report. Whether true or not, it was inevitable. Kikuchiyo was merely the one who happened to be on hand when the moment arrived.

Quite aware that his indignation might be comical, Kawase was taken with another impulse, to have a try at seeing where the indignation would lead him. In fact it was for a time like the first touch of ardour he had known. He was rather pleased.

But Asaka's response was wholly unacceptable. After his own wilful fashion, he had thought that, as she had responded to his jokes with jokes of her own, so she would respond to this first show of ardour with ardour of her own. Hating to be the only comical one, he had hoped that the woman too would give herself up to the comedy and answer with appropriate excitement.

Stubbornly silent, she sat with almost excessive propriety by the window of the snack bar, almost empty in the mid-afternoon lull. The silence seemed to Kawase evidence of obtuseness. She had not seen that his excitement amounted to a first avowal of love.

He had expected to see unconcealed pleasure come into her eyes at his persistent accusations. All his troublesome pride seemed to hang on it. If he could but see the pleasure, he would forgive her everything.

It was not long before Kawase had said all he had to say and they both fell silent, avoiding each other's eyes. It was a cloudy autumn afternoon. The streets below were crowded. The dust-covered neon tubes of the cabaret across the way could be studied in great detail.

Asaka looked stubbornly out of the window. Without the slightest change of expression, she began to weep. She scarcely moved her lips as she said: 'I think I'm going to have a baby. Your baby.'

That single remark made Kawase, who had not thought of leaving her, decide to do just that. What a cheap trick! All memory of the brisk, clean affair seemed to vanish, fallen into the dirty world of bargaining and haggling. He did not even feel like saying what most men would have said, that there was no way of knowing whose child it was. He said it all the same, very clearly, with an eye on what was to come later. If she wanted a bout of mud-slinging, he would give her what she asked for. For the first time Kawase found himself disliking those dance-like gestures, the thick, white, professional make-up. They had seemed like the essence of the elegant and the stylish, but now they were only symbols of vulgarity and lack of sensitivity. He was glad that her insincerity had made up his mind for him.

'As a matter of fact, my own boy ...' Although Asaka perhaps did not guess the content of the remarks he was on the verge of making, she may have sensed that he was in danger of saying something better left unsaid. She stopped him in the Western manner, with a light, somewhat intoxicated wink.

It was nicely timed. The fact that he was stopped not by himself but by her brought a strange, sweet, melting emotion.

'And did you enjoy the cherries jubilee?' asked the waiter.

Kawase had intended to leave a 15-per-cent tip, but he left a 20-per-cent tip instead.

5

During the twelve-hour jet flight back to Japan, Kawase went time after time to the lounge for a smoke and thought of the bright morning light in his hotel, where Asaka had stayed the night.

With a shortage of help to look after the hundreds of rooms, the rule that a guest could not have a woman in his room, current in all good hotels, had become an empty form. Outside the elevator the hotel corridor was empty late at night. There was not even a danger of being overheard, walking along the thick carpeting under rows of old-fashioned brackets. Somewhat befuddled, Asaka and Kawase bet five dollars on whether or not they could get in a dozen kisses between the elevator and the room, a considerable distance away. Kawase won.

In the morning they awoke from a brief sleep, drew back the curtains, and looked far down at San Francisco Bay, shimmering between buildings in the morning sunlight.

The day before, having breakfast alone, Kawase had scattered crumbs to the pigeons on the ledge. They flew up again this morning when he opened the window. There were no crumbs today, however, for the two of them could scarcely call for room service. Disappointed, the pigeons withdrew to a hollow below the ledge, craned their necks inquiringly for a time, and flew away. Their necks were an intricate combination of blue, brown, and green.

Below, the cable car was already clanging its way up the street. Asaka was in a black slip, her rich shoulders bare. It was flesh with which he had long been familiar, and yet, here abroad, it seemed to give off a strong, simple scent as of the meadows, quite the opposite of the artificial scent it had in kimono and powder. That the earthiness in her skin, like the effect of the sun sinking into the skins of her ancestors over the ages, should give such pleasure to a person whose skin was the same colour was one of those strange reversals possible only in a foreign country.

It was a fine, free morning, and all the bonds and restraints that had tied Kawase's heart from the morning before were miraculously swept away.

Bringing the neck of his pyjamas together against the morning chill, he said brightly: 'And what will you do this time if you have a baby?'

Asaka was seated like a foreign prostitute at the mirror, dazzling in the sunlight. She was looking at her reflection. The gentle slope of the shoulders seemed to send out its own radiance.

'If I have a baby it will be Sonoda's,' she answered, briskly mentioning the name of her patron.

But as he approached Japan, that memory faded and the image of his wife and child in their loneliness grew stronger. Kawase did not himself know why he seemed so intent upon painting them in sad, sentimental colours. Was there some force that drove him to look upon them so? His wife had written faithfully once a week in his absence, and her letters indicated that all was well.

The jet flew low over the sea. The lights were turned out to show the lights of Tokyo, and soft music played. The plane would apparently go directly into Haneda Airport from the bay off Yokohama. Clusters of lights came slowly up at them. All the strained sadness of the city – the more people crowded into it the more sadness – seemed to be in those clusters of lights.

In the heady disquiet of returning home from a long trip abroad, Kawase listened to the deep breathing of the engines and gave himself up to the precise and yet somehow frustrating flow of time and space as rows of lights at the runways emerged from the disorder.

The confusion of customs, the irritation of waiting for his luggage – performing the last duties required of the traveller at the end of the road, he climbed the red-carpeted stairs and immediately saw his wife, child in arms, among the welcomers. She had on a lawn-green sweater and she had gained weight in his absence. The outline of her face was somehow blurred, making her if anything more attractive.

'See? There's papa,' she said to the child, who hung impassively on her neck, worn out by the crowd and the excitement. At length, as if he could think of no alternative, he wrinkled his nose and smiled.

There was nothing lonely or unhappy about them. The signs were that they had been quite content in Kawase's absence. He was disappointed that his wife should be so bright and cheerful.

Several of his subordinates went with them to his house for a home-coming party. Kawase had no chance to talk to his wife.

The child was nodding at his knee.

'Maybe he should go to bed,' said one of the men from the office.

Amid the appurtenances of Japan – straw mats, sliding paper doors, alcove, round window, countless little dishes and decanters on the table – Kawase had become the classical Japanese gentleman once more. He had to assert his authority.

'If you show him a thermos flask, he'll be wide awake again.'

'A thermos flask?'

'Kimiko,' Kawase called to his wife, 'bring a thermos flask.'

She was slow to answer. No doubt she agreed that it was time the boy was in bed. It was after eleven. Her evasiveness greatly irritated Kawase. It came to seem that he had returned to Japan solely for the pleasure of accosting the child with a thermos flask. It was as if only that feeling of pleasure or fear, he scarcely knew which, could clear away the disquiet deep inside him since the jet flight.

Five minutes later he called to his wife again. Intoxication did not spread pleasantly as it should, but seemed to form a cold lump at the back of his head.

'What about the thermos flask?'

'Yes.'

'But see how sleepy he is,' said Komiya, the same young man. 'I think we can do without the thermos flask.'

Emboldened by sake, Komiya was being somewhat forward. Kawase glanced at him. He was a very intelligent young man, one of the best in Kawase's section, and he had a distinctive face, thick eyebrows that came faintly together over the bridge of the nose. Catching the man's eye, Kawase felt something stab at the icy lump in his head: He knows. He knows the boy's afraid of thermos flasks.

Instead of asking why, Kawase shoved the child at Komiya, who caught it as if it were a football and looked at Kawase in frank amazement.

'You put him to bed, then,' said Kawase.

Sensing that it was a dangerous moment, the others became even noisier. Kawase's wife slipped in, took the child from Komiya, and went off to put it to bed, almost asleep despite the clamour. The smoothness of the operation did not please Kawase.

It was one o'clock by the time the guests left.

Kawase helped his wife clear the table. Though exhausted, he felt more awake than ever and not in the least intoxicated. His displeasure seemed to have made itself known to his wife. They exchanged as few words as possible while they were engaged in this small cooperative task.

'Thank you very much. Why don't you go to bed? You must be tired.' Splashing at the dish-washer, she did not look round.

Kawase did not answer. The dishes of left-overs by the sink were starkly white in the fluorescent light.

After a time he said: 'What about the thermos flask? I knew he was sleepy, but you could have brought it on my first night home.'

'It's broken.' Over the sound of the water his wife answered in a bright, unnaturally high voice.

It was odd that Kawase did not find the news surprising.

'Who broke it? Shigeru?'

She shook her head. The stiff, heaped-up waves of hair, reset for his home-coming, shook softly.

'Who did break it, then?'

She had been washing dishes, but suddenly her arms were motionless, and he sensed that she had them braced against the stainless steel of the sink as if pushing at it. The lawn-green sweater was shaking.

'But what is there to cry about? I just asked you who broke it.'

'I broke it,' she said in little gasps.

Kawase did not have the courage to lay his hand on her shoulder. He was afraid of thermos flasks.

Translated by Edward G. Seidensticker

The Priest of Shiga Temple and His Love

According to Eshin's 'Essentials of Salvation', the Ten Pleasures are but a drop in the ocean when compared to the joys of the Pure Land. In the Land the earth is made of emerald and the roads that lead across it are lined by cordons of gold rope. The surface is endlessly level and there are no boundaries. Within each of the sacred Precincts are fifty thousand million halls and towers wrought of gold, silver, lapis lazuli, crystal, coral, agate, and pearls; and wondrous garments are spread out on all the jewelled daisies. Within the halls and above the towers a multitude of angels are for ever playing sacred music and singing paeans of praise to the Tathagata Buddha. In the gardens that surround the halls and the towers and the cloisters are great gold and emerald ponds where the faithful may perform their ablutions; and the gold ponds are lined with silver sand, and the emerald ponds are lined with crystal sand. The ponds are covered with lotus plants which sparkle in variegated colours and, as the breeze wafts over the surface of the water, magnificent lights crisscross in all directions. Both day and night the air is filled with the songs of cranes, geese, mandarin ducks, peacocks, parrots, and sweet-voiced Kalavinkas, who have the faces of beautiful women. All these and the myriad other hundred-jewelled birds are raising their melodious voices in praise of the Buddha. (However sweet their voices may sound, so immense a collection of birds must be extremely noisy.)

The borders of the ponds and the banks of the rivers are lined with groves of sacred treasure trees. These trees have golden stems and silver branches and coral blossoms, and their beauty is mirrored in the waters. The air is full of jewelled cords, and from these cords hang the myriad treasure bells which for ever ring out the Supreme Law of Buddha; and strange musical instruments, which play by themselves without ever being touched, also stretch far into the pellucid sky.

If one feels like having something to eat, there automatically appear before one's eyes a seven-jewelled table on whose shining surface rest seven-jewelled bowls heaped high with the choicest delicacies. But there is no need to pick up these viands and put them in one's mouth. All that is necessary is to look at their inviting colours and to enjoy the aroma: thereby the stomach is filled and the body nourished, while one remains oneself spiritually and physically pure. When one has thus finished one's meal without any eating, the bowls and the table are instantly wafted off.

Likewise, one's body is automatically arrayed in clothes, without any need for sewing, laundering, dyeing, or repairing.

Lamps, too, are unnecessary, for the sky is illumined by an omnipresent light. Furthermore, the Pure Land enjoys a moderate temperature all year round, so that neither heating nor cooling is required. A hundred thousand subtle scents perfume the air and lotus petals rain down constantly.

In the chapter of the Inspection Gate we are told that, since uninitiated sightseers cannot hope to penetrate deep into the Pure Land, they must concentrate, first, on awakening their powers of 'external imagination' and, thereafter, on steadily expanding these powers. Imaginative power can provide a short cut for escaping from the trammels of our mundane life and for seeing the Buddha. If we are endowed with a rich, turbulent imagination, we can focus our attention on a single lotus flower and from there can spread out to infinite horizons.

By means of microscopic observation and astronomical projection the lotus flower can become the foundation for an entire theory of the universe and an agent whereby we may perceive the Truth. And first we must know that each of the petals has eighty-four thousand veins and that each vein gives off eighty-four thousand lights. Furthermore, the smallest of these flowers has a diameter of two hundred and fifty yojana. Thus, assuming that the yojana of which we read in the Holy Writings correspond to seventy-five miles each, we may conclude that a lotus flower with a diameter of nineteen thousand miles is on the small side.

Now such a flower has eighty-four thousand petals and between each of the petals there are one million jewels, each emitting one thousand lights. Above the beautifully adorned calyx of the flower rise four bejewelled pillars and each of these pillars is one hundred billion times as great as Mount Sumeru, which towers in the centre of the Buddhist universe. From the pillars hang great draperies and each drapery is adorned with fifty thousand million jewels, and each jewel emits eighty-four thousand lights, and each light is composed of eighty-four thousand different golden colours, and each of these golden colours in its turn is variously transmogrified.

To concentrate on such images is known as 'thinking of the Lotus Seat on which Lord Buddha sits'; and the conceptual world that hovers in the background of our story is a world imagined on such a scale.

The Great Priest of Shiga Temple was a man of the most eminent virtue. His eyebrows were white, and it was as much as he could do to move his old bones along as he hobbled on his stick from one part of the temple to another.

In the eyes of this learned ascetic the world was a mere pile of rubbish. He had lived away from it for many a long year and the little pine sapling that he had planted with his own hands on moving into his present cell had grown into a great tree whose branches swelled in the wind. A monk who had succeeded in abandoning the Floating World for so long a time must feel secure about his future.

When the Great Priest saw the rich and the noble, he smiled with compassion and wondered how it was that these people did not recognize their pleasures for the empty dreams that they were. When he noticed beautiful women, his only reaction was to be moved with pity for men who still inhabited the world of delusion and who were tossed about on the waves of carnal pleasure.

From the moment that a man no longer responds in the slightest to the motives that regulate the material world, that world appears to be at complete repose. In the eyes of the Great Priest the world showed only repose; it had become a mere picture on a piece of paper, a map of some foreign land. When one has attained a state of mind from which the evil passions of the present world have been so utterly winnowed, fear too is forgotten. Thus it was that the priest no longer could understand why Hell should exist. He knew beyond all peradventure that the present world no longer had any power left over him; but, as he was completely devoid of conceit, it did not occur to him that this was the effect of his own eminent virtue.

So far as his body was concerned, one might say that the priest had well-nigh been deserted by his own flesh. On such occasions as he observed it – when taking a bath, for instance – he would rejoice to see how his protruding bones were precariously covered by his withered skin. Now that his body had reached this stage, he felt that he could come to terms with it, as if it belonged to someone else. Such a body, it seemed, was already more suited for the nourishment of the Pure Land than for terrestrial food and drink.

In his dreams he lived nightly in the Pure Land, and when he awoke he knew that to subsist in the present world was to be tied to a sad and evanescent dream.

In the flower-viewing season large numbers of people came from the Capital to visit the village of Shiga. This did not trouble the priest in the slightest, for he had long since transcended that state in which the clamours of the world can irritate the mind. One spring evening he left his cell, leaning on his stick, and walked down to the lake. It was the hour when dusky shadows slowly begin to thrust their way into the bright light of the afternoon. There was not the slightest ripple to disturb the surface of the water. The priest stood by himself at the edge of the lake and began to perform the holy rite of Water Contemplation.

At that moment an ox-drawn carriage, clearly belonging to a person of high rank, came round the lake and stopped close to where the priest was standing. The owner was a Court lady from the Kyōgoku district of the Capital who held the exalted title of Great Imperial Concubine. This lady had come to view the springtime scenery in Shiga and now on her return she had stopped the carriage and raised the blind in order to have a final look at the lake.

Unwittingly the Great Priest glanced in her direction and at once he was overwhelmed by her beauty. His eyes met hers, and he did nothing to avert his gaze, she did not take it upon herself to turn away. It was not that her liberality of spirit was such as to allow men to gaze on her with brazen looks; but the motives of this austere old ascetic could hardly, she felt, be those of ordinary men.

After a few moments the lady pulled down the blind. Her carriage started to move and, having gone through the Shiga Pass, rolled slowly down the road that led to the Capital. Night fell and the carriage made its way towards the city along the Road of the Silver Temple. Until the carriage had become a pinprick that disappeared between the distant trees, the Great Priest stood rooted to the spot.

In the twinkling of an eye, the present world had wreaked its revenge on the priest with terrible force. What he had imagined to be completely safe had collapsed in ruins.

He returned to the temple, faced the Main Image of Buddha, and invoked the Sacred Name. But impure thoughts now cast their opaque shadows about him. A woman's beauty, he told himself, was but a fleeting apparition, a temporary phenomenon composed of flesh – of flesh that was soon to be destroyed. Yet, try as he might to ward it off, the ineffable beauty which had overpowered him at that instant by the lake now pressed on his heart with the force of something that has come from an infinite distance. The Great Priest was not young enough, either spiritually or physically, to believe that this new feeling was simply a trick that his flesh had played on him. A man's flesh, he knew full well, could not alter so rapidly. Rather, he seemed to have been immersed in some swift, subtle poison which had abruptly transmuted his spirit.

The Great Priest had never broken his vow of chastity. The inner fight that he had waged in his youth against the demands of the flesh had made him think of women as mere carnal beings. The only real flesh was the flesh that existed in his imagination. Since, therefore, he regarded the flesh as an ideal abstraction, rather than as a physical fact, he had relied on his spiritual strength to subjugate it. In this effort the priest had achieved success – success, indeed, that no one who knew him could possibly doubt.

Yet the face of the woman who had raised the carriage blind and gazed across the lake was too harmonious, too refulgent, to be designated as a mere object of flesh, and the priest did not know what name to give it. He could only think that, in order to bring about that wondrous moment, something which had for a long time lurked deceptively within him had finally revealed itself. That thing was nothing other than the present world, which until then had been at repose, but which had now suddenly lifted itself out of the darkness and begun to stir.

It was as if he had been standing by the highway that led to the Capital, with his hands firmly covering both ears, and had watched two great oxcarts rumble past each other. All of a sudden he had removed his hands and the noise from outside had surged all about him.

To perceive the ebb and flow of passing phenomena, to have their noise roaring in one's ears, was to enter into the circle of the present world. For a man like the Great Priest, who had severed his relations with all outside things, it was to place himself once again into a state of relationship.

Even as he read the Sutras he would time after time hear himself heaving great sighs of anguish. Perhaps nature, he thought, might serve to distract his spirits, and he gazed out of the window of his cell at the mountains that towered in the distance under the evening sky. Yet his thoughts, instead of concentrating on the beauty, broke up like tufts of cloud and drifted away. He fixed his gaze on the moon, but his thoughts continued to wander as before; and when once again he went and stood before the Main Image in a desperate effort to regain his purity of mind, the countenance of the Buddha was transformed and looked like the face of the lady in the carriage. His universe had been imprisoned within the confines of a small circle: at one point was the Great Priest and opposite was the Great Imperial Concubine.

The Great Imperial Concubine of Kyōgoku had soon forgotten about the old priest whom she had noticed gazing so intently at her by the lake at Shiga. After some time, however, a rumour came to her ears and she was reminded of the incident. One of the villagers happened to have caught sight of the Great Priest as he had stood watching the lady's carriage disappear into the distance. He had mentioned the matter to a Court gentleman who had come to Shiga for flower-viewing and had added that since that day the priest had behaved like one crazed.

The Imperial Concubine pretended to disbelieve the rumour. The virtue of this particular priest, however, was noted throughout the Capital, and the incident was bound to feed the lady's vanity.

For she was utterly weary of the love that she received from the men of this world. The Imperial Concubine was fully aware of her own beauty, and she tended to be attracted by any force, such as religion, that treated her beauty and her high rank as things of no value. Being exceedingly bored with the present world, she believed in the Pure Land. It was inevitable that Jōdo Buddhism, which rejected all the beauty and brilliance of the visual world as being mere filth and defilement, should have a particular appeal for someone like the Imperial Concubine who was thoroughly disillusioned with the superficial elegance of Court life – an elegance that seemed unmistakably to bespeak the Latter Days of the Law and their degeneracy.

Among those whose special interest was love, the Great Imperial Concubine was held in honour as the very personification of Courtly refinement. The fact that she was known never to have given her love to any man added to this reputation. Though she performed her duties towards the Emperor with the most perfect decorum, no one for a moment believed that she loved him from her heart. The Great Imperial Concubine dreamt of a passion that lay on the boundary of the impossible.

The Great Priest of Shiga Temple was famous for his virtue, and everyone in the Capital knew how this aged prelate had totally abandoned the present world. All the more startling, then, was the rumour that he had been dazzled by the charms of the Imperial Concubine, and that for her sake he had sacrificed the future world. To give up the joys of the Pure Land which were so close at hand – there could be no greater sacrifice than this, no greater gift.

The Great Imperial Concubine was utterly indifferent to the charms of the young rakes who flocked about the Court and of the handsome noblemen who came her way. The physical attributes of men no longer meant anything to her. Her only concern was to find a man who could give her the strongest and deepest possible love. A woman with such aspirations is a truly terrifying creature. If she is a mere courtesan, she will no doubt be satisfied with worldly wealth. The Great Imperial Concubine, however, already enjoyed all those things that the wealth of the world can provide. The man whom she awaited must offer her the wealth of the future world.

The rumours of the Great Priest's infatuation spread throughout the Court. In the end the story was even told half-jokingly to the Emperor himself. The Great Concubine took no pleasure in this bantering gossip and preserved a cool, indifferent mien. As she was well aware, there were two reasons why the people of the Court could joke freely about a matter which would normally have been forbidden: first, by referring to the Great Priest's love they were paying a compliment to the beauty of the woman who could inspire even an ecclesiastic of such great virtue to forsake his meditations; secondly, everyone fully realized that the old man's love for the noblewoman could never possibly be requited.

The Great Imperial Concubine called to mind the face of the old priest whom she had seen through her carriage window. It did not bear the remotest resemblance to the face of any of the men who had loved her until then. Strange it was that love should spring up in the heart of a man who did not have the slightest qualification for being loved. The lady recalled such phrases as 'my love forlorn and without hope' that were widely used by poetasters in the Palace when they wished to awaken some sympathy in the hearts of their indifferent paramours. Compared to the hopeless situation in which the Great Priest now found himself, the state of the least fortunate of these elegant lovers was almost enviable, and their poetic tags struck her now as mere trappings of worldly alliance, inspired by vanity and utterly devoid of pathos.

At this point it will be clear to the reader that the Great Imperial Concubine was not, as was so widely believed, the personification of Courtly elegance, but, rather, a person who found the real relish of life in the knowledge of being loved. Despite her high rank, she was first of all a woman; and all the power and authority in the world seemed to her empty things if they were bereft of this knowledge. The men about her might devote themselves to struggles for political power; but she dreamt of subduing the world by different means, by purely feminine means. Many of the women whom she had known had taken the tonsure and retired from the world. Such women struck her as laughable. For, whatever a woman may say about abandoning the world, it is almost impossible for her to give up the things that she possesses. Only men are really capable of giving up what they possess.

That old priest by the lake had at a certain stage in his life given up the Floating World and all its pleasures. In the eyes of the Imperial Concubine he was far more of a man than all the nobles whom she knew at Court. And, just as he had once abandoned this present Floating World, so now on her behalf he was about to give up the future world as well.

The Imperial Concubine recalled the notion of the sacred lotus flower, which her own deep faith had vividly imprinted upon her mind. She thought of the huge lotus with its width of two hundred and fifty yojana. That preposterous plant was far more fitted to her tastes than those puny lotus flowers which floated on the ponds in the Capital. At night when she listened to the wind soughing through the trees in the garden, the sound seemed to her extremely insipid when compared to the delicate music in the Pure Land when the wind blew through the sacred treasure trees. When she thought of the strange instruments that hung in the sky and that played by themselves without ever being touched, the sound of the harp that echoed through the Palace halls seemed to her a paltry imitation.

The Great Priest of Shiga Temple was fighting. In the fight that he had waged against the flesh in his youth he had always been buoyed up by the hope of inheriting the future world. But this desperate fight of his old age was linked with a sense of irreparable loss.

The impossibility of consummating his love for the Great Imperial Concubine was as clear to him as the sun in the sky. At the same time he was fully aware of the impossibility of advancing towards the Pure Land so long as he remained in the thralls of this love. The Great Priest, who had lived in an incomparably free state of mind, had in a twinkling been enclosed in darkness and the future was totally obscure. It may have been that the courage which had seen him through his youthful struggles had grown out of self-confidence and pride in the fact that he was voluntarily depriving himself of pleasure that could have been his for the asking.

The Great Priest was again possessed by fear. Until that noble carriage had approached the side of Lake Shiga, he had believed that what lay in wait for him, close at hand, was nothing less than the final release of Nirvana. But now he had awakened into the darkness of the present world, where it is impossible to see what lurks a single step ahead.

The various forms of religious meditation were all in vain. He tried the Contemplation of the Chrysanthemum, the Contemplation of the Total Aspect, and the Contemplation of the Parts; but each time that he started to concentrate, the beautiful visage of the Concubine appeared before his eyes. Water Contemplation, too, was useless, for invariably her lovely face would float up shimmering from beneath the ripples of the lake.

This, no doubt, was a natural consequence of his infatuation. Concentration, the priest soon realized, did more harm than good, and next he tried to dull his spirit by dispersal. It astonished him that spiritual concentration should have the paradoxical effect of leading him still deeper into his delusions; but he soon realized that to try the contrary method of dispersing his thoughts meant that he was, in effect, admitting these very delusions. As his spirit began to yield under the weight, the priest decided that, rather than pursue a futile struggle, it were better to escape from the effort of escaping by deliberately concentrating his thoughts on the figure of the Great Imperial Concubine.

The Great Priest found a new pleasure in adorning his vision of the lady in various ways, just as though he were adorning a Buddhist statue with diadems and baldachins. In so doing, he turned the object of his love into an increasingly resplendent, distant, impossible being; and this afforded him particular joy. But why? Surely it would be more natural for him to envisage the Great Imperial Concubine as an ordinary female, close at hand and possessing normal human frailties. Thus he could better turn her to advantage, at least in his imagination.

As he pondered this question, the truth dawned on him. What he was depicting in the Great Imperial Concubine was not a creature of flesh, nor was it a mere vision; rather, it was a symbol of reality, a symbol of the essence of things. It was strange, indeed, to pursue that essence in the figure of a woman. Yet the reason was not far to seek. Even when falling in love, the Great Priest of Shiga had not discarded the habit, to which he had trained himself during his long years of contemplation, of striving to approach the essence of things by means of constant abstraction. The Great Imperial Concubine of Kyōgoku had now become uniform with his vision of the immense lotus of two hundred and fifty yojana. As she reclined on the water supported by all the lotus flowers, she had become vaster than Mount Sumeru, vaster than an entire realm.

The more the Great Priest turned his love into something impossible, the more deeply was he betraying the Buddha. For the impossibility of this love had become bound up with the impossibility of attaining enlightenment. The more he thought of his love as hopeless, the firmer grew the fantasy that supported it and the deeper-rooted became his impure thoughts. So long as he regarded his love as being even remotely feasible, it was paradoxically possible for him to resign himself; but now that the Great Concubine had grown into a fabulous and utterly unattainable creature the priest's love became motionless like a great stagnant lake which firmly, obdurately, covers the earth's surface.

He hoped that somehow he might see the lady's face once more, yet he feared that when he met her, that figure, which had now become like a giant lotus, would crumble away without a trace. If that were to happen, he would without doubt be saved. Yes, this time he was bound to attain enlightenment. And the very prospect filled the Great Priest with fear and awe.

The priest's lonely love had begun to devise strange, self-deceiving guiles, and when at length he reached the decision to go and see the lady, he was under the delusion that he had almost recovered from the illness that was searing his body. The bemused priest even mistook the joy that accompanied his decision for relief at having finally escaped from the trammels of his love.

None of the Great Concubine's people found anything especially strange in the sight of an old priest standing silently in the corner of the garden, leaning on a stick and gazing sombrely at the residence. Ascetics and beggars frequently stood outside the great houses of the Capital and waited for alms. One of the ladies in attendance mentioned the matter to her mistress. The Great Imperial Concubine casually glanced through the blind that separated her from the garden. There in the shadow of the fresh green foliage stood a withered old priest with faded black robes and bowed head. For some time the lady looked at him. When she realized that this was without any question the priest whom she had seen by the lake at Shiga, her pale face turned paler still.

After a few moments of indecision, she gave orders that the priest's presence in her garden should be ignored. Her attendants bowed and withdrew.

Now for the first time the lady fell prey to uneasiness. In her lifetime she had seen many people who had abandoned the world, but never before had she laid eyes on someone who had abandoned the future world. The sight was ominous and inexpressibly fearful. All the pleasure that her imagination had conjured up from the idea of the priest's love disappeared in a flash. Much as he might have surrendered the future world on her behalf, that world, she now realized, would never pass into her own hands.

The Great Imperial Concubine looked down at her elegant clothes and at her beautiful hands, and then she looked across the garden at the uncomely features of the old priest and at his shabby robes. There was a horrible fascination in the fact that a connection should exist between them.

How different it all was from the splendid vision! The Great Priest seemed now like a person who had hobbled out of Hell itself. Nothing remained of that man of virtuous presence who had trailed the brightness of the Pure Land behind him. The brilliance which had resided within him and which had called to mind the glory of the Pure Land had vanished utterly. Though this was certainly the man who had stood by the Shiga Lake, it was at the same time a totally different person.

Like most people of the Court, the Great Imperial Concubine tended to be on her guard against her own emotions, especially when she was confronted with something that could be expected to affect her deeply. Now on seeing this evidence of the Great Priest's love, she felt disheartened at the thought that the consummate passion of which she had dreamt during all these years should assume so colourless a form.

When the priest had finally limped into the Capital leaning on his stick, he had almost forgotten his exhaustion. Secretly he made his way into the grounds of the Great Imperial Concubine's residence at Kyōgoku and looked across the garden. Behind those blinds, he thought, was sitting none other than the lady whom he loved.

Now that his adoration had assumed an immaculate form, the future world once again began to exert its charm on the Great Priest. Never before had he envisaged the Pure Land in so immaculate, so poignant, an aspect. His yearning for it became almost sensual. Nothing remained for him but the formality of meeting the Great Concubine, of declaring his love, and of thus ridding himself once and for all of the impure thoughts that tied him to this world and that still prevented him from attaining the Pure Land. That was all that remained to be done.

It was painful for him to stand there supporting his old body on his stick. The bright rays of the May sun poured through the leaves and beat down on his shaven head. Time after time he felt himself losing consciousness and without his stick he would certainly have collapsed. If only the lady would realize the situation and invite him into her presence, so that the formality might be done with! The Great Priest waited. He waited and supported his ever-growing weariness on his stick. At length the sun was covered with the evening clouds. Dusk gathered. Yet still no word came from the Great Imperial Concubine.

She, of course, had no way of knowing that the priest was looking through her, beyond her, into the Pure Land. Time after time she glanced out through the blinds. He was standing there immobile. The evening light thrust its way into the garden. Still he continued standing there.

The Great Imperial Concubine became frightened. She felt that what she saw in the garden was an incarnation of that 'deep-rooted delusion' of which she had read in the Sutras. She was overcome by the fear of tumbling into Hell. Now that she had led astray a priest of such high virtue, it was not the Pure Land to which she could look forward, but Hell itself, whose terrors she and those about her knew in such detail. The supreme love of which she had dreamt had already been shattered. To be loved as she was – that in itself represented damnation. Whereas the Great Priest looked beyond her into the Pure Land, she now looked beyond the priest into the horrid realms of Hell.

Yet this haughty noblewoman of Kyōgoku was too proud to succumb to her fears without a fight, and she now summoned forth all the resources of her inbred ruthlessness. The Great Priest, she told herself, was bound to collapse sooner or later. She looked through the blind, thinking that by now he must be lying on the ground. To her annoyance, the silent figure stood there motionless.

Night fell and in the moonlight the figure of the priest looked like a pile of chalk-white bones.

The lady could not sleep for fear. She no longer looked through the blind and she turned her back to the garden. Yet all the time she seemed to feel the piercing gaze of the Great Priest on her back.

This, she knew, was no commonplace love. From fear of being loved, from fear of falling into Hell, the Great Imperial Concubine prayed more earnestly than ever for the Pure Land. It was for her own private Pure Land that she prayed – a Pure Land which she tried to preserve invulnerable within her heart. This was a different Pure Land from the priest's and it had no connection with his love. She felt sure that if she were ever to mention it to him it would instantly disintegrate.

The priest's love, she told herself, had nothing to do with her. It was a one-sided affair, in which her own feelings had no part, and there was no reason why it should disqualify her from being received into her Pure Land. Even if the Great Priest were to collapse and die, she would remain unscathed. Yet, as the night advanced and the air became colder, this confidence began to desert her.

The priest remained standing in the garden. When the moon was hidden by the clouds, he looked like a strange, gnarled old tree.

That form out there has nothing to do with me, thought the lady, almost beside herself with anguish, and the words seemed to boom within her heart. Why in Heaven's name should this have happened?

At that moment, strangely, the Great Imperial Concubine completely forgot about her own beauty. Or perhaps it would be more correct to say that she had made herself forget it.

Finally, faint traces of white began to break through the dark sky and the priest's figure emerged in the dawn twilight. He was still standing. The Great Imperial Concubine had been defeated. She summoned a maid and told her to invite the priest to come in from the garden and to kneel outside her blind.

The Great Priest was at the very boundary of oblivion when the flesh is on the verge of crumbling away. He no longer knew whether it was for the Great Imperial Concubine that he was waiting or for the future world. Though he saw the figure of the maid approaching from the residence into the dusky garden, it did not occur to him that what he had been waiting for was finally at hand.

The maid delivered her mistress's message. When she had finished, the priest uttered a dreadful, almost inhuman cry. The maid tried to lead him by the hand, but he pulled away and walked by himself towards the house with fantastically swift, firm steps.

It was dark on the other side of the blind and from outside it was impossible to see the lady's form. The priest knelt down and, covering his face with his hands, he wept. For a long time he stayed there without a word and his body shook convulsively.

Then in the dawn darkness a white hand gently emerged from behind the lowered blind. The priest of the Shiga Temple took it in his own hands and pressed it to his forehead and cheek.

The Great Imperial Concubine of Kyōgoku felt a strange cold hand touching her hand. At the same time she was aware of a warm moisture. Her hand was being bedewed by someone else's tears. Yet when the pallid shafts of morning light began to reach her through the blind, the lady's fervent faith imbued her with a wonderful inspiration: she became convinced that the unknown hand which touched hers belonged to none other than the Buddha.

Then the great vision sprang up anew in the lady's heart: the emerald earth of the Pure Land, the millions of seven-jewelled towers, the angels playing music, the golden ponds strewn with silver sand, the resplendent lotus, and the sweet voices of the Kalavinkas – all this was born afresh. If this was the Pure Land that she was to inherit – and so she now believed – why should she not accept the Great Priest's love?

She waited for the man with the hands of Buddha to ask her to raise the blind that separated her from him. Presently he would ask her; and then she would remove the barrier and her incomparably beautiful body would appear before him as it had on that day by the edge of the lake at Shiga; and she would invite him to come in.

The Great Imperial Concubine waited.

But the priest of Shiga Temple did not utter a word. He asked her for nothing. After a while his old hands relaxed their grip and the lady's snow-white hand was left alone in the dawn light. The priest departed. The heart of the Great Imperial Concubine turned cold.

A few days later a rumour reached the Court that the Great Priest's spirit had achieved its final liberation in his cell at Shiga. At this news the lady of Kyōgoku set to copying the Sutras in roll after roll of beautiful writing.

Translated by Ivan Morris

The Seven Bridges

At half past eleven on the night of the September full moon, as soon as the party at which they had been entertaining broke up, Koyumi and Kanako returned to the Laurel House and at once slipped into cotton kimonos. They would really have preferred to bathe before setting out again, but they had no time tonight.

Koyumi was forty-two, a plump little figure, barely five feet tall, wrapped in a white kimono patterned with black leaves. Kanako, the other geisha, though only twenty-two and quite a good dancer, had no patron and seemed fated never to be assigned a decent part in the annual spring and autumn geisha dances. Her crepe kimono was dyed dark-blue whirls on white.

Kanako spoke. 'I wonder what design Masako's kimono will be tonight?'

'Clover, you can be sure. She's desperate to have a baby.'

'Has she gone that far, then?'

'That's the trouble – she hasn't,' Koyumi answered. 'She's still a long way from success. What a Virgin Mary that'd make her – getting a baby from a man simply from having a crush on him!' – There is a common superstition among the geishas that a woman who wears a summer kimono with a clover pattern or a winter kimono with a landscape design will soon become pregnant.

When at last they were ready to leave, Koyumi felt the sudden pangs of hunger. It happened every time she set out on the evening's round of parties, but she felt as if hunger were always an unexpected catastrophe striking without warning from the blue. She was never bothered by hunger while appearing before customers, no matter how boring the party might be, but, before and after she performed, the hunger which she had quite forgotten would assail her like a sudden fit. Koyumi could never prepare for this eventuality by eating appropriately at a suitable time. Sometimes, for example, when she went in the evening to the hairdresser, she would see the other geishas of the neighbourhood ordering a meal and eating it with relish as they waited their turn. But the sight produced no impression on Koyumi. She didn't even think that the *risotto*, or whatever the dish was, might taste good. And yet, an hour later, hunger pangs would suddenly strike, and the saliva would gush like a hot spring from the roots of her small, strong teeth.

Koyumi and Kanako paid a monthly bill to the Laurel House for publicity and for their meals. Koyumi's meal bill had always been exceptionally large. Not only was she a heavy eater, but she was finicky in her tastes. But, as a matter of fact, ever since she developed her eccentric habit of feeling hungry only before and after appearances, her food bill had gradually been decreasing, and it threatened now to drop below Kanako's. Koyumi had no recollection of when this eccentric habit had originated, nor of when she first made it her practice to stop by the kitchen before the first party of the evening to demand, all but dancing with impatience, 'Haven't you a little something I can eat?' It was now her custom to take her dinner in the kitchen of the first house, and her supper in the kitchen of the last house of the evening. Her stomach had attuned itself to this routine, and her food bill at the Laurel House had accordingly dwindled.

The Ginza was already deserted as the two geisha started walking towards the Yonei House in Shimbashi. Kanako pointed up at the sky over a bank with metal blinds barring the windows. 'We're lucky it's clear, aren't we? You can really see the man in the moon tonight.'

Koyumi's thoughts were only for her stomach. Her first party tonight had been at Yonei's and her last at the Fuminoya. She realized now that she should have eaten supper at the Fuminoya before starting out, but there had been no time. She had rushed right back to the Laurel House to change. She would have to ask for supper at their destination, Yonei's, in the same kitchen where she had eaten dinner that evening. The thought weighed on her.

But Koyumi's anxiety was dispelled as soon as she stepped inside the kitchen door at Yonei's. Masako, the much-sheltered daughter of the owner, was standing by the entrance waiting for them. She wore the clover-patterned kimono which they had predicted. Seeing Koyumi, she tactfully called out, 'I didn't expect you so soon. We're in no hurry – come in and have a bit of supper before you go.'

The kitchen was littered with odds and ends from the evening's entertainments. Enormous stacks of plates and bowls glared in the unshaded electric lights. Masako stood with one hand braced against the frame of the door, her body blocking the light and her face dark in the shadows. The light did not reach Koyumi's face, and she was glad that her momentary expression of relief when Masako called to her had passed unnoticed.

While Koyumi was eating supper, Masako led Kanako to her room. Of all the geisha who came to the Yonei House, Kanako was the one she got along with best. She and Masako were the same age, had gone to elementary school together, and were about equally good-looking. But, more important than any of these reasons, the fact was that she somehow liked Kanako.

Kanako was so demure she looked as if the least wind would blow her over, but she had accumulated all the experience she needed, and a carelessly uttered word from her sometimes did Masako a world of good. The high-spirited Masako, on the other hand, was timid and childish when it came to love. Her childishness was a matter of common gossip, and her mother was so sure of the girl's innocence that she had not given it a second thought when Masako ordered a kimono with a clover design.

Masako was a student in the Arts Department at Waseda University. She had always been an admirer of R, the movie actor, but ever since he had visited Yonei's her passion for him had been mounting. Her room was now cluttered with pictures of him. She had ordered a white china vase enamelled with the photograph of R and herself taken on the memorable occasion of his visit. It stood on her desk, filled with flowers.

Kanako said when she was seated, 'They announced the cast today.' She twisted her thin little mouth into a frown.

'Did they?' Masako, sorry for Kanako, pretended not to know.

'All I got was a bit part again. I'll never get anything better. It's enough to discourage me for good. I feel like a girl in a musical who stays in the chorus year after year.'

'I'm sure you'll get a good part next year.'

Kanako shook her head. 'In the meantime I'm getting old. Before you know it, I'll be like Koyumi.'

'Don't be silly. You've still got twenty years ahead of you.'

It would not have been proper in the course of this conversation for either girl to mention what she would be praying for tonight, but even without asking each already knew the other's prayers. Masako wanted an affair with R; Kanako a good patron; and they both knew that Koyumi wanted money.

Their prayers, it was clear, would have quite different objects, all eminently reasonable. If the moon failed to grant these wishes, the moon and not they would be at fault. Their hopes showed plainly and honestly on their faces, and theirs were such truly human desires that anyone seeing the three women walking in the moonlight would surely be convinced that the moon would have no choice but to recognize their sincerity and grant their wishes.

Masako spoke. 'We'll have one more coming along tonight.'

'Not really? Who?'

'A maid. Her name's Mina, and she came from the country a month ago. I told Mother I didn't want her coming with me, but Mother said she'd worry if she didn't send somebody along.'

Kanako asked, 'What's she like?'

'Just wait till you see her. She's what you'd call well-developed.'

At that moment Mina opened the sliding doors behind them and, still standing, poked in her head.

'I thought I told you that when you open sliding doors you're supposed to kneel down first and then open them.' Masako's tone was haughty.

'Yes, miss.' Mina's coarse, heavy voice seemed to reflect nothing of Masako's feelings. Kanako had to restrain a laugh at Mina's appearance. She wore a one-piece dress made up of strange bits and patches of kimono material. Her hair was set in a rumpled permanent wave, and her extraordinarily brawny arms showing through her sleeves rivalled her face in duskiness. Her heavy features were crushed under the swollen mass of her cheeks, and her eyes were like slits. No matter which way she chose to shut her mouth, one or another of her irregular teeth protruded. It was difficult to uncover any expression in that face.

'Quite a bodyguard!' Kanako murmured into Masako's ear.

Masako forced a severe expression to her face. 'You're sure you understand? I've told you already, but I'll tell you once more. From the minute we set foot out of this house you're not to open your mouth, no matter what happens, until we've crossed all seven bridges. Even one word and you won't get whatever you're praying for. And if anybody you know talks to you, you're out of luck, but I don't suppose there's much danger of that in your case. One more thing. You're not allowed to go back over the same road twice. Anyway, Koyumi will be leading. All you have to do is follow.'

At the university Masako had to submit reports on the novels of Marcel Proust, but when it came to matters of this nature the modern education she had received at school deserted her completely.

'Yes, miss,' Mina answered. It was by no means clear whether or not she had actually understood.

'You've got to come along anyway; you might as well make a wish. Have you thought of something?'

'Yes, miss,' Mina said, a smile slowly spreading over her face.

'Why, she acts like everybody else!' commented Kanako.

Koyumi appeared at that moment, cheerfully patting her midriff. 'I'm all set now.'

'Have you picked good bridges for us?' asked Masako.

'We'll start with Miyoshi Bridge. It goes over two rivers, so it counts as two bridges. Doesn't that make things easier? Pretty clever of me, if I must say so.'

The three women, aware that once they stepped outside they would be unable to utter another word, began to talk loudly and all at once, as if to discharge a great accumulation of chatter. The chatter continued until they had reached the kitchen door. Masako's black-lacquered geta were waiting for her on the earthen floor by the door. As her bare feet stepped into the geta, her polished and manicured toenails gave off a a lustre faintly visible in the dark. Koyumi exclaimed, 'That's real style! Nail rouge and black geta – not even the moon can resist you now!'

' "Nail rouge!" That dates you, Koyumi!'

'I know the word. "Mannequin", isn't it?'

Masako and Kanako, exchanging glances, burst out laughing.

The four women stepped out on to Showa Avenue, Koyumi leading them. They passed a parking lot where a great many taxis, their work ended for the day, reflected the moonlight from their black chassis. The cries of insects could be heard from under the cars. Traffic was still heavy on Showa Avenue, but the street itself was fast asleep, and the roar of passing motor-cycles sounded lonely and isolated without the accompaniment of the usual street noises.

A few scraps of cloud drifted in the sky under the moon, now and then touching the heavy bank of cloud girdling the horizon. The moon shone unobscured. At breaks in the traffic noises the clatter of their geta seemed to rebound straight from the pavement to the hard blue surface of the sky.

Koyumi walking ahead of the others, was pleased that only a broad, deserted street lay before her. It was Koyumi's boast that she had always got along without depending on anyone, and she was glad that her stomach was full. She couldn't understand as she walked happily along why she was so anxious to have more money. Koyumi felt as if her real wish was to melt gently and meaninglessly into the moonlight falling on the pavement ahead of her. Splinters of glass glittered in cracks in the sidewalk. Even bits of glass could glitter in the moonlight – it made her wonder if her long-standing wish were not something like that broken glass.

Masako and Kanako, their little fingers hooked, trod on the long shadow Koyumi trailed behind her. The night air was cool, and they both felt the faint breeze penetrate their sleeves, chilling and tightening their breasts damp with perspiration from excitement over their departure. Through linked fingers their prayers were communicated, the more eloquently because no words were spoken.

Masako was picturing to herself R's sweet voice, his long, finely drawn eyes, his locks curling under the temples. She, the daughter of the owner of a first-class restaurant in Shimbashi, was not to be lumped together with his other fans – she saw no reason why her prayer could not be granted. She remembered that when R spoke, his breath, falling on her ear, had been fragrant, not smelling in the least of liquor. She remembered that young, manly breath, heavy with the sultriness of summer hay. If such recollections came to her when she was alone, she felt something like a ripple of water slide over her skin from her knees to the thighs. She was as certain – yet as uncertain – that R's body existed somewhere in the world of the accuracy of her recurring memories. The element of doubt constantly tortured her.

Kanako was dreaming of a rich, fat, middle-aged man. He would have to be fat or he wouldn't really seem rich. How happy she would be, she thought, if she could shut her eyes and feel herself engulfed by his generous, unstinted protection! Kanako was accustomed to shutting her eyes, but her experience up to now had been that when she opened them again the man in question had disappeared.

The two girls looked back over their shoulders, as if by common consent. Mina was silently trudging behind them. Her hands pressed to her cheeks, she was grotesquely lurching along, kicking up the hems of her dress at each step. Her eyes stared vacantly into space, devoid of any purpose. Masako and Kanako felt that Mina's appearance constituted an insult to their prayers.

They turned right on Showa Avenue, just where the first and second wards of the East Ginza meet. Light from street lamps fell like splashes of water at regular intervals along the row of buildings. Shadows hid the moonlight from the narrow street.

Soon they could see Miyoshi Bridge rising before them, the first of the seven bridges they were to cross. It is built in a curious Y-shape because of the fork in the river at this spot. The gloomy buildings of the Central District Office squatted on the opposite bank, the white face of a clock in its tower proclaiming an absurdly incorrect hour against the dark sky. Miyoshi Bridge has a low railing, and at each of the corners of the central section, where the three arms of the bridge meet, stands an old-fashioned lamp post hung with a cluster of electric lights. Each cluster has four lamps, but not all were lit, and the unlit globes shone a dead white in the moonlight. Swarms of winged insects flocked silently round the lamps.

The water in the river was ruffled by the moonlight.

At the end of the bridge, before they crossed it, the women, led by Koyumi, joined their hands in prayer. A dim light went out in the window of a small building near by, and a man, apparently leaving after finishing his overtime work, the last to leave, emerged from the building. He started to lock the door when he noticed the strange spectacle and stopped in his tracks.

The women gradually began to cross the bridge. It was hardly more than a continuation of the pavement over which they had been striding so confidently, but, faced with their first bridge, their steps became heavy and uncertain, as though they were stepping on to a stage. It was only a few feet to the other side of the first arm of the bridge, but those few feet brought a sense of accomplishment and relief.

Koyumi paused under a lamp post and, looking back at the others, joined her hands in prayer again. The three women imitated her. According to Koyumi's calculations, crossing two of the three arms of the bridge would count as crossing two independent bridges. This meant that they would have to pray four times on Miyoshi Bridge, once before and after crossing each arm.

Masako noticed, when an occasional taxi passed, the astonished faces of the passengers pressed against the windows, but Koyumi paid no attention to such things.

The women, having arrived before the District Office, turned their backs to it and prayed for the fourth time. Kanako and Masako began to feel, along with relief at having safely crossed the first two bridges, that the prayers which they had not taken very seriously until now represented something of irreplaceable importance.

Masako had come to feel that she would rather be dead if she couldn't be with R. The mere act of crossing two bridges had multiplied many times the strength of her desires. Kanako was now convinced that life would not be worth living if she couldn't find a good patron. Their hearts swelled with emotion as they prayed, and Masako's eyes suddenly grew warm.

She happened to glance to her side. Mina, her eys shut, was reverently joining her hands. Masako was sure that Mina's prayer, whatever it was, could not be as important as her own. She felt scorn and also envy for the empty, insensible cavern in Mina's heart.

They walked south, following the river as far as the streetcar line. The last car had, of course, departed long ago, and the rails which by day burned with early autumn sunlight now stretched out two white, cool lines.

Even before they reached the streetcar line Kanako had begun to feel strange pains in her abdomen. Something she ate must have disagreed with her. The first slight symptoms of a wrenching pain were forgotten two or three steps farther on, followed by recurring sensations of relief that she had forgotten the pain, but a crack developed in this reassurance, and even while she was telling herself that she had forgotten the pain, it began to reassert itself.

Tsukiji Bridge was the third. They noticed at the end of this bleak-looking bridge in the heart of the city a willow-tree, faithfully planted in the traditional manner. A forlorn willow that they normally would never have noticed as they sped past it in a car grew from a tiny patch of earth at a break in the concrete. Its leaves, faithful to tradition, trembled in the river breeze. Late at night the noisy buildings around it died, and only this willow went on living.

Koyumi, standing in the shadow of the willow, joined her hands in prayer before crossing Tsukiji Bridge. It may have been her sense of responsibility as the leader which made Koyumi's plump little figure stand unusually erect. As a matter of fact, Koyumi had long since forgotten what she was praying for. The important thing ahead of her now, she thought, was to cross the seven bridges without major mishap. This determination to cross the bridges, no matter what happened, was, she felt, a sign that crossing the bridges had itself become the object of her prayers. This was a very peculiar outlook, but she realized that it,. like her sudden seizures of hunger, belonged to her way of life, a reflection which hardened into a strange conviction as she walked in the moonlight. Her back was held straighter than ever, her eyes looked directly before her.

Tsukiji Bridge is a bridge utterly without charm. The four stone pillars marking the ends are equally unattractive. But as the women crossed the bridge they could smell for the first time something like the odour of the sea, and a wind reminiscent of a salt breeze was blowing. Even the red neon sign of an insurance company, visible to the south farther down the river, looked to them like a beacon warning of the steady approach of the sea.

They crossed the bridge and prayed again. Kanako felt that her pain, now acute, was making her sick. They crossed the streetcar line and walked between the old yellow buildings of the S Enterprises and the river. Kanako gradually began to fall behind. Masako, worried, also slowed her pace, but unfortunately she could not open her mouth to ask if Kanako was all right. Kanako finally made her understand by pressing her hands against her abdomen and grimacing with pain.

Koyumi, in something like a state of inebriation, continued to march triumphantly ahead at her usual pace, unaware that anything had happened. The distance between her and the others widened.

Now, when a fine patron loomed before her eyes, so close she need only reach out her hands to grab him, Kanako realized helplessly that her hands would never stretch far enough. Her face had turned deathly pale, and a greasy sweat oozed from her forehead. The human heart, however, is surprisingly adaptable: as the pain in her abdomen grew more intense, Kanako's wish, so ardently desired a moment before, her prayer which had seemed so close to fulfilment, somehow lost all reality, and she came to feel that it had been from the start an unrealistic, fantastic, and childish dream. She felt as she struggled painfully ahead, fighting the relentless, throbbing pain, that if only she gave up her foolish delusion her pain would immediately be healed.

When at last the fourth bridge came into sight, Kanako laid her hand lightly on Masako's shoulder, and, in something like the gesture language of the dance, she pointed to her stomach and shook her head. The stray locks plastered with perspiration against her cheeks seemed to say that she could go no farther. She turned abruptly on her heels and dashed back towards the streetcar line.

Masako's first impulse was to run after Kanako, but, remembering that her prayer would be nullified if she turned back, she checked herself and merely watched Kanako run. Koyumi first realized that something was amiss when she reached the bridge. By then Kanako was running frantically in the moonlight, not caring how she looked. Her blue-and-white kimono flapped, and the sound of her geta echoed and scattered against the nearby buildings. A lone taxi could be seen, providentially parked at the corner.

The fourth bridge was Irifuna Bridge. They would cross it in the direction opposite to that they had taken over Tsukiji Bridge.

The three women gathered at the end of the bridge and prayed with identical motions. Masako was sorry for Kanako, but her pity did not well up as spontaneously as usual. What passed through her head instead was the cold reflection that anyone who dropped from the ranks would henceforth travel a path different from her own. Each woman's prayer was her own problem, and even in such an emergency Masako could not be expected to shoulder anyone else's burden. It would not be helping someone to carry a heavy load up a mountain – it would be doing something which could not be of use to anyone.

The name 'Irifuna Bridge' was written in white letters on a horizontal metal plaque fastened to a post at the end of the bridge. The bridge itself stood out in the dark, its concrete surface caught in the merciless glare reflected from the Caltex petrol station on the opposite bank. A little light could be seen in the river where the bridge cast its shadow. The man who lived in the broken-down hut at the end of the fishing-pier was apparently still up, and the light belonged to him. His hut was decorated with potted plants and a sign announcing: 'Pleasure Boats, Tow Boats, Fishing Boats, Netting Boats.'

The roof line of the crowded range of buildings across the river gradually dropped off, and the night sky seemed to open before them. They noticed now that the moon, so bright a little while earlier, was only translucently visible through thin clouds. All over the sky the clouds had gathered.

The women crossed Irifuna Bridge without incident.

Beyond Irifuna Bridge the river bends almost at a right angle. The fifth bridge was quite a distance away. They would have to follow the river along the wide, deserted embankment to Akatsuki Bridge.

Most of the buildings to their right were restaurants. To their left on the river bank were piles of stone, gravel, and sand for some sort of construction project, the dark mass spilling at places half-way over the roadway. Before long, the imposing buildings of St Luke's Hospital could be seen to their left across the river. The hospital bulked gloomily in the hazy moonlight. The huge gold cross on top was brightly illuminated, and the red lights of aeroplane beacons, as if in attendance on the cross, flashed from rooftops here and there, demarcating the roofs and the sky. The lights were out in the chapel behind the hospital, but the outlines of its Gothic rose window were plainly visible. In the hospital windows a few dim lights were still burning.

The three women walked on in silence. Masako, her mind absorbed by the task ahead of her, could think of little else. Their pace had imperceptibly quickened until she was now damp with perspiration. Then – at first she thought it must be imagination – the sky, in which the moon was still visible, grew threatening, and she felt the first drops of rain against her forehead. Fortunately, however, the rain showed no signs of developing into a downpour.

Now Akatsuki Bridge, their fifth, loomed ahead. The concrete posts, whitewashed for some unknown reason, shone a ghostly colour in the dark. As Masako joined her hands in prayer at the end of the bridge, she tripped and almost fell on an exposed iron pipe in the roadway. Across the bridge was the streetcar turn before St. Luke's Hospital.

The bridge was not long. The women were walking so quickly that they were across it almost immediately, but on the other side Koyumi met with misfortune. A woman with her hair let down after washing and a metal basin in her hand approached from the opposite direction. She was walking quickly, her kimono opened in slatternly fashion off the shoulders. Masako caught only a glimpse of the woman, but the deadly pallor of the face under the wet hair made her shudder.

The woman stopped on the bridge and turned back. 'Why, if it isn't Koyumi! It's been ages, hasn't it? Are you pretending you don't know me? Koyumi – you remember me!' She craned her neck at Koyumi, blocking her path. Koyumi lowered her eyes and did not answer. The woman's voice was high-pitched and unfocused, like the wind escaping through a crevice. Her prolonged monotone suggested that she was calling not Koyumi but someone who wasn't actually there. 'I'm just on my way back from the bath-house. It's really been ages. Of all places to meet!'

Koyumi, feeling the woman's hand on her shoulder, finally opened her eyes. She realized that it was useless to begrudge the woman an answer – the fact that she had been addressed by an acquaintance was enough to destroy her prayer.

Masako looked at the woman's face. She thought for a moment, then walked on, leaving Koyumi behind. Masako remembered the woman's face. She was an old geisha who had appeared for a while in Shimbashi just after the war – Koen was her name. She had become rather peculiar, acting like a teenage girl despite her age, and she finally had been removed from the register of geisha. It was not surprising that Koen had recognized Koyumi, an old friend, but it was a stroke of good fortune that she should have forgotten Masako.

The sixth bridge lay directly ahead, Sakai Bridge, a small structure marked only by a metal sign painted green. Masako hurried through her prayers at the foot of the bridge and all but raced across. When she looked back she noticed to her relief that Koyumi was no longer to be seen. Directly behind her followed Mina, her face maintaining its usual sullen expression.

Now that she was deprived of her guide, Masako had no clue where to find the seventh and last bridge. She reasoned, however, that if she kept going along the same street she would sooner or later come to a bridge parallel to Akatsuki Bridge. She would only have to cross the final bridge for her prayers to be answered.

A sprinkling of raindrops again struck Masako's face. The road ahead was lined with wholesale warehouses, and construction shacks blocked her view of the river. It was very dark. Bright street lamps in the distance made the darkness in between seem all the blacker. Masako was not especially afraid to walk through the streets so late at night. She had an adventurous nature and her goal, the accomplishment of her prayer, lent her courage. But the sound of Mina's geta echoing behind her began to hang like a heavy pall on Masako. The sound actually had a cheerful irregularity, but the utter self-possession of Mina's gait, as contrasted with her own mincing steps, seemed to be pursuing Masako with its derision.

Until Kanako dropped from the ranks, Mina's presence had merely aroused a kind of contempt in Masako's heart, but since then it had come somehow to weigh on her, and now that there were only two of them left, Masako could not help being bothered, despite herself, by the riddle of what this girl from the backwoods could possibly be praying for. It was disagreeable to have this stolid woman with her unfathomable prayers treading in her footsteps. No, it was not so much unpleasant as disquieting, and Masako's uneasiness gradually mounted until it was close to terror.

Masako had never realized how upsetting it was not to know what another person wanted. She felt there was something like a lump of blackness following her, not at all like Kanako or Koyumi, whose prayers had been so transparently clear she could see through them. Masako tried desperately to arouse her longings for R to an even more feverish pitch than before. She thought of his face. She thought of his voice. She remembered his youthful breath. But the image shattered at once, and she did not attempt to restore it.

She must get over the seventh bridge as quickly as possible. Until then she would not think about anything.

The street lamps she had seen from the distance now began to look like the lights at the end of a bridge. She could tell that she was approaching a main thoroughfare, and there were signs that a bridge could not be far off.

First came a little park, where the street lights she had seen from the distance shone down on the black dots the rain was splashing into a sand pile, then the bridge itself, its name 'Bizen Bridge' inscribed on a concrete pillar at the end. A single bulb at the top of the pillar gave off a feeble light. Masako saw to her right, across the river, the Tsukiji Honganji Temple, its curved green roof rising into the night sky. She recognized the place. She would have to be careful once she crossed the bridge not to pass over the same route on her way back home.

Masako breathed a sigh of relief. She joined her hands in prayer at the end of the bridge and, to make up for her perfunctory performances before, this time she prayed carefully and devoutly. Out of the corner of her eye she could see Mina, aping her as usual, piously pressing together her thick palms. The sight so annoyed Masako as to deflect her prayer somehow from its real object, and the words which kept rising to her lips were, 'I wish I hadn't brought her along. She's really exasperating. I should never have brought her.'

Just then a man's voice called out to Masako. She felt her body go rigid. A patrolman stood by her. His young face was tense and his voice sounded shrill. 'What are you doing here – at this time of night, in a place like this?'

Masako could not answer. One word would ruin everything. She realized immediately from the policeman's breathless questioning and the tone of his voice that he had mistakenly supposed that the girl praying on a bridge in the middle of the night intended to throw herself into the river. Masako could not speak. She would have to make Mina understand that she must answer instead. She tugged at Mina's dress and tried to awaken her intelligence. No matter how obtuse Mina might be, it was inconceivable that she should fail to understand, but she kept her mouth obstinately shut. Masako saw to her dismay that – whether in obedience to the original instructions or because she intended to protect her own prayer – Mina was resolved not to speak.

The policeman's tone became rougher. 'Answer me. I want an answer.'

Masako decided that her best bet was to make a break for the other side of the bridge and to explain once she was across. She shook off the policeman's hand and raced out on to the bridge. Even as Masako started running, she noticed Mina dash out after her.

About half-way across the bridge the policeman caught up with Masako. He grabbed her arm. 'Tried to run away, did you?'

'Run away? What a thing to say! You're hurting me, holding my arm like that!' Masako cried out before she knew it. Then, realizing that her prayers had been brought to nothing, she glared at the other end of the bridge, her eyes burning with fury. Mina, safely across, was completing the fourteenth and last prayer.

Masako complained hysterically to her mother when she got

home, and the other, not knowing what it was all about, scolded Mina. 'What were you praying for, anyway?' she asked Mina.

Mina only smirked for an answer.

A few days later Masako, her spirits somewhat revived, was teasing Mina. She asked for the hundredth time, 'What were you praying for? Tell me. Surely you can tell me now.'

Mina only gave a faint and evasive smile.

'You're dreadful! Mina, you're really dreadful!'

Masako laughingly poked Mina's shoulder with the sharp points of her manicured nails. The resilient, heavy flesh repelled the nails. A dull sensation lingered in Masako's fingertips, and she felt at a loss what to do with her hand.

Translated by Donald Keene

Patriotism

On the twenty-eighth of February, 1936 (on the third day, that is, of the February 26 Incident), Lieutenant Shinji Takeyama of the Konoe Transport Battalion – profoundly disturbed by the knowledge that his closest colleagues had been with the mutineers from the beginning, and indignant at the imminent prospect of Imperial troops attacking Imperial troops – took his officer's sword and ceremonially disembowelled himself in the eight-mat room of his private residence in the sixth block of Aoba-chō, in Yotsuya Ward. His wife, Reiko, followed him, stabbing herself to death. The lieutenant's farewell note consisted of one sentence: 'Long live the Imperial Forces.' His wife's, after apologies for her unfilial conduct in thus preceding her parents to the grave, concluded: 'The day which, for a soldier's wife, had to come, has come. . . .' The last moments of this heroic and dedicated couple were such as to make the gods themselves weep. The lieutenant's age, it should be noted, was thirty-one, his wife's twenty-three; and it was not half a year since the celebration of their marriage.

Those who saw the bride and bridegroom in the commemorative photograph – perhaps no less than those actually present at the lieutenant's wedding – had exclaimed in wonder at the bearing of this handsome couple. The lieutenant, majestic in military uniform, stood protectively beside his bride, his right hand resting upon his sword, his officer's cap held at his left side. His expression was severe, and his dark brows and wide-gazing eyes well conveyed the clear integrity of youth. For the beauty of the bride in her white over-robe no comparisons were adequate. In the eyes, round beneath soft brows, in the slender, finely shaped nose, and in the full lips, there was both sensuousness and refinement. One hand, emerging shyly from a sleeve of the over-robe, held a fan, and the tips of the fingers, clustering delicately, were like the bud of a moonflower.

After the suicide, people would take out this photograph and examine it, and sadly reflect that too often there was a curse on these seemingly flawless unions. Perhaps it was no more than imagination, but looking at the picture after the tragedy it almost seemed as if the two young people before the gold-lacquered screen were gazing, each with equal clarity, at the deaths which lay before them.

Thanks to the good offices of their go-between, Lieutenant General Ozeki, they had been able to set themselves up in a new home at Aoba-chō in Yotsuya. 'New home' is perhaps misleading. It was an old three-room rented house backing on to a small garden. As neither the six- nor the four-and-a-half-mat room downstairs was favoured by the sun, they used the upstairs eight-mat room as both bedroom and guest room. There was no maid, so Reiko was left alone to guard the house in her husband's absence.

The honeymoon trip was dispensed with on the grounds that these were times of national emergency. The two of them had spent the first night of their marriage at this house. Before going to bed, Shinji, sitting erect on the floor with his sword laid before him, had bestowed upon his wife a soldierly lecture. A woman who had become the wife of a soldier should know and resolutely accept that her husband's death might come at any moment. It could be tomorrow. It could be the day after. But, no matter when it came – he asked – was she steadfast in her resolve to accept it? Reiko rose to her feet, pulled open a drawer of the cabinet, and took out what was the most prized of her new possessions, the dagger her mother had given her. Returning to her place, she laid the dagger without a word on the mat before her, just as her husband had laid his sword. A silent understanding was achieved at once, and the lieutenant never again sought to test his wife's resolve.

In the first few months of her marriage Reiko's beauty grew daily more radiant, shining serene like the moon after rain.

As both were possessed of young, vigorous bodies, their relationship was passionate. Nor was this merely a matter of the night. On more than one occasion, returning home straight from manoeuvres, and begrudging even the time it took to remove his mud-splashed uniform, the lieutenant had pushed his wife to the floor almost as soon as he had entered the house. Reiko was equally ardent in her response. For a little more or a little less than a month, from the first night of their marriage Reiko knew happiness, and the lieutenant, seeing this, was happy too.

Reiko's body was white and pure, and her swelling breasts conveyed a firm and chaste refusal; but, upon consent, those breasts were lavish with their intimate, welcoming warmth. Even in bed these two were frighteningly and awesomely serious. In the very midst of wild, intoxicating passions, their hearts were sober and serious.

By day the lieutenant would think of his wife in the brief rest periods between training; and all day long, at home, Reiko would recall the image of her husband. Even when apart, however, they had only to look at the wedding photograph for their happiness to be once more confirmed. Reiko felt not the slightest surprise that a man who had been a complete stranger until a few months ago should now have become the sun about which her whole world revolved.

All these things had a moral basis, and were in accordance with the Education Rescript's injunction that 'husband and wife should be harmonious'. Not once did Reiko contradict her husband, nor did the lieutenant ever find reason to scold his wife. On the god shelf below the stairway, alongside the tablet from the Great Ise Shrine, were set photographs of their Imperial Majesties, and regularly every morning, before leaving for duty, the lieutenant would stand with his wife at this hallowed place and together they would bow their heads low. The offering water was renewed each morning, and the sacred sprig of *sasaki* was always green and fresh. Their lives were lived beneath the solemn protection of the gods and were filled with an intense happiness which set every fibre in their bodies trembling.

2

Although Lord Privy Seal Saitō's house was in their neighbourhood, neither of them heard any noise of gunfire on the morning of 26 February. It was a bugle, sounding muster in the dim, snowy dawn, when the ten-minute tragedy had already ended, which first disrupted the lieutenant's slumbers. Leaping at once from his bed, and without speaking a word, the lieutenant donned his uniform, buckled on the sword held ready for him by his wife, and hurried swiftly out into the snow-covered streets of the still darkened morning. He did not return until the evening of the twenty-eighth.

Later, from the radio news, Reiko learned the full extent of this sudden eruption of violence. Her life throughout the subsequent two days was lived alone, in complete tranquillity, and behind locked doors.

In the lieutenant's face, as he hurried silently out into the snowy morning, Reiko had read the determination to die. If her husband did not return, her own decision was made: she too would die. Quietly she attended to the disposition of her personal possessions. She chose her sets of visiting kimonos as keepsakes for friends of her schooldays, and she wrote a name and address on the stiff paper wrapping in which each was folded. Constantly admonished by her husband never to think of the morrow, Reiko had not even kept a diary and was now denied the pleasure of assiduously rereading her record of the happiness of the past few months and consigning each page to the fire as she did so. Ranged across the top of the radio were a small china dog, a rabbit, a squirrel, a bear, and a fox. There were also a small vase and a water pitcher. These comprised Reiko's one and only collection. But it would hardly do, she imagined, to give such things as keepsakes. Nor again would it be quite proper to ask specifically for them to be included in the coffin. It seemed to Reiko, as these thoughts passed through her mind, that the expressions on the small animals' faces grew even more lost and forlorn.

Reiko took the squirrel in her hand and looked at it. And then, her thoughts turning to a realm far beyond these childlike affections, she gazed up into the distance at the great sunlike principle which her husband embodied. She was ready, and happy, to be hurtled along to her destruction in that gleaming sun chariot – but now, for these few moments of solitude, she allowed herself to luxuriate in this innocent attachment to trifles. The time when she had genuinely loved these things, however, was long past. Now she merely loved the memory of having once loved them, and their place in her heart had been filled by more intense passions, by a more frenzied happiness. . . . For Reiko had never, even to herself, thought of those soaring joys of the flesh as a mere pleasure. The February cold, and the icy touch of the china squirrel, had numbed Reiko's slender fingers; yet, even so, in her lower limbs, beneath the ordered repetition of the pattern which crossed the skirt of her trim *meisen* kimono, she could feel now, as she thought of the lieutenant's powerful arms reaching out towards her, a hot moistness of the flesh which defied the snows.

She was not in the least afraid of the death hovering in her mind. Waiting alone at home, Reiko firmly believed that everything her husband was feeling or thinking now, his anguish and distress, was leading her – just as surely as the power in his flesh – to a welcome death. She felt as if her body could melt away with ease and be transformed to the merest fraction of her husband's thought.

Listening to the frequent announcements on the radio, she heard the names of several of her husband's colleagues mentioned among those of the insurgents. This was news of death. She followed the developments closely, wondering anxiously, as the situation became daily more irrevocable, why no Imperial ordinance was sent down, and watching what had at first been taken as a movement to restore the nation's honour come gradually to be branded with the infamous name of mutiny. There was no communication from the regiment. At any moment, it seemed, fighting might commence in the city streets, where the remains of the snow still lay.

Towards sunset on the twenty-eighth Reiko was startled by a furious pounding on the front door. She hurried downstairs. As she pulled with fumbling fingers at the bolt, the shape dimly outlined beyond the frosted-glass panel made no sound, but she knew it was her husband. Reiko had never known the bolt on the sliding door to be so stiff. Still it resisted. The door just would not open.

In a moment, almost before she knew she had succeeded, the lieutenant was standing before her on the cement floor inside the porch, muffled in a khaki greatcoat, his top boots heavy with slush from the street. Closing the door behind him, he returned the bolt once more to its socket. With what significance, Reiko did not understand.

'Welcome home.'

Reiko bowed deeply, but her husband made no response. As he had already unfastened his sword and was about to remove his greatcoat, Reiko moved round behind to assist. The coat, which was cold and damp and had lost the odour of horse dung it normally exuded when exposed to the sun, weighed heavily upon her arm. Draping it across a hanger, and cradling the sword and leather belt in her sleeves, she waited while her husband removed his top boots and then followed behind him into the 'living-room'. This was the six-mat room downstairs.

Seen in the clear light from the lamp, her husband's face, covered with a heavy growth of bristle, was almost unrecognizably wasted and thin. The cheeks were hollow, their lustre and resilience gone. In his normal good spirits he would have changed into old clothes as soon as he was home and have pressed her to get supper at once, but now he sat before the table still in his uniform, his head drooping dejectedly. Reiko refrained from asking whether she should prepare the supper.

After an interval the lieutenant spoke.

'I knew nothing. They hadn't asked me to join. Perhaps out of consideration, because I was newly married. Kanō, and Homma too, and Yamaguchi.'

Reiko recalled momentarily the faces of high-spirited young officers, friends of her husband, who had come to the house occasionally as guests.

'There may be an Imperial ordinance sent down tomorrow. They'll be posted as rebels, I imagine. I shall be in command of a unit with orders to attack them. ... I can't do it. It's impossible to do a thing like that.'

He spoke again.

'They've taken me off guard duty, and I have permission to return home for one night. Tomorrow morning, without question, I must leave to join the attack. I can't do it, Reiko.'

Reiko sat erect with lowered eyes. She understood clearly that her husband had spoken of his death. The lieutenant was resolved. Each word, being rooted in death, emerged sharply and with powerful significance against this dark, unmovable background. Although the lieutenant was speaking of his dilemma, already there was no room in his mind for vacillation.

However, there was a clarity, like the clarity of a stream fed from melting snows, in the silence which rested between them. Sitting in his own home after the long two-day ordeal, and looking across at the face of his beautiful wife, the lieutenant was for the first time experiencing true peace of mind. For he had at once known, though she said nothing, that his wife divined the resolve which lay beneath his words.

'Well, then ...' The lieutenant's eyes opened wide. Despite his exhaustion they were strong and clear, and now for the first time they looked straight into the eyes of his wife. 'Tonight I shall cut my stomach.'

Reiko did not flinch.

Her round eyes showed tension, as taut as the clang of a bell.

'I am ready,' she said. 'I ask permission to accompany you.'

The lieutenant felt almost mesmerized by the strength in those eyes. His words flowed swiftly and easily, like the utterances of a man in delirium, and it was beyond his understanding how permission in a matter of such weight could be expressed so casually.

'Good. We'll go together. But I want you as a witness, first, for my own suicide. Agreed?'

When this was said a sudden release of abundant happiness welled up in both their hearts. Reiko was deeply affected by the greatness of her husband's trust in her. It was vital for the lieutenant, whatever else might happen, that there should be no irregularity in his death. For that reason there had to be a witness. The fact that he had chosen his wife for this was the first mark of his trust. The second, and even greater mark, was that though he had pledged that they should die together he did not intend to kill his wife first – he had deferred her death to a time when he would no longer be there to verify it. If the lieutenant had been a suspicious husband, he would doubtless, as in the usual suicide pact, have chosen to kill his wife first.

When Reiko said, 'I ask permission to accompany you,' the lieutenant felt these words to be the final fruit of the education which he had himself given his wife, starting on the first night of their marriage, and which had schooled her, when the moment came, to say what had to be said without a shadow of hesitation. This flattered the lieutenant's opinion of himself as a self-reliant man. He was not so romantic or conceited as to imagine that the words were spoken spontaneously, out of love for her husband.

With happiness welling almost too abundantly in their hearts, they could not help smiling at each other. Reiko felt as if she had returned to her wedding night.

Before her eyes was neither pain nor death. She seemed to see only a free and limitless expanse opening out into vast distances.

'The water is hot. Will you take your bath now?'

'Ah yes, of course.'

'And supper . . .?'

The words were delivered in such level, domestic tones that the lieutenant came near to thinking, for the fraction of a second, that everything had been a hallucination.

'I don't think we'll need supper. But perhaps you could warm some sake?'

'As you wish.'

As Reiko rose and took a *tanzen* gown from the cabinet for after the bath, she purposely directed her husband's attention to the opened drawer. The lieutenant rose, crossed to the cabinet, and looked inside. From the ordered array of paper wrappings he read, one by one, the addresses of the keepsakes. There was no grief in the lieutenant's response to this demonstration of heroic resolve. His heart was filled with tenderness. Like a husband who is proudly shown the childish purchases of a young wife, the lieutenant, overwhelmed by affection, lovingly embraced his wife from behind and implanted a kiss upon her neck.

Reiko felt the roughness of the lieutenant's unshaven skin against her neck. This sensation, more than being just a thing of this world, was for Reiko almost the world itself, but now – with the feeling that it was soon to be lost for ever – it had freshness beyond all her experience. Each moment had its own vital strength, and the senses in every corner of her body were reawakened. Accepting her husband's caresses from behind, Reiko raised herself on the tips of her toes, letting the vitality seep through her entire body.

'First the bath, and then, after some sake . . . lay out the bedding upstairs, will you?'

The lieutenant whispered the words into his wife's ear. Reiko silently nodded.

Flinging off his uniform, the lieutenant went to the bath. To faint background noises of slopping water Reiko tended the charcoal brazier in the living-room and began the preparations for warming the sake.

Taking the *tanzen*, a sash, and some underclothes, she went to the bathroom to ask how the water was. In the midst of a coiling cloud of steam the lieutenant was sitting cross-legged on the floor, shaving, and she could dimly discern the rippling movements of the muscles on his damp, powerful back as they responded to the movement of his arms.

There was nothing to suggest a time of any special significance. Reiko, going busily about her tasks, was preparing side dishes from odds and ends in stock. Her hands did not tremble. If anything, she managed even more efficiently and smoothly than usual. From time to time, it is true, there was a strange throbbing deep within her breast. Like distant lightning, it had a moment of sharp intensity and then vanished without trace. Apart from that, nothing was in any way out of the ordinary.

The lieutenant, shaving in the bathroom, felt his warmed body miraculously healed at last of the desperate tiredness of the days of indecision and filled – in spite of the death which lay ahead – with pleasurable anticipation. The sound of his wife going about her work came to him faintly. A healthy physical craving, submerged for two days, reasserted itself.

The lieutenant was confident there had been no impurity in the joy they had experienced when resolving upon death. They had both sensed at that moment – though not, of course, in any clear and conscious way – that those permissible pleasures which they shared in private were once more beneath the protection of Righteousness and Divine Power, and of a complete and unassailable morality. On looking into each other's eyes and discovering there an honourable death, they had felt themselves safe once more behind steel walls which none could destroy, encased in an impenetrable armour of Beauty and Truth. Thus, so far from seeing any inconsistency or conflict between the surges of his flesh and the sincerity of his patriotism, the lieutenant was even able to regard the two as parts of the same thing.

Thrusting his face close to the dark, cracked, misted wall-mirror, the lieutenant shaved himself with great care. This would be his death face. There must be no unsightly blemishes. The clean-shaven face gleamed once more with a youthful lustre, seeming to brighten the darkness of the mirror. There was a certain elegance, he even felt, in the association of death with this radiantly healthy face.

Just as it looked now, this would become his death face! Already, in fact, it had half departed from the lieutenant's personal possession and had become the bust above a dead soldier's memorial. As an experiment he closed his eyes tight. Everything was wrapped in blackness, and he was no longer a living, seeing creature.

Returning from the bath, the traces of the shave glowing faintly blue beneath his smooth cheeks, he seated himself beside the now well-kindled charcoal brazier. Busy though Reiko was, he noticed, she had found time lightly to touch up her face. Her cheeks were gay and her lips moist. There was no shadow of sadness to be seen. Truly, the lieutenant felt, as he saw this mark of his young wife's passionate nature, he had chosen the wife he ought to have chosen.

As soon as the lieutenant had drained his sake cup he offered it to Reiko, Reiko had never before tasted sake, but she accepted without hesitation and sipped timidly.

'Come here,' the lieutenant said.

Reiko moved to her husband's side and was embraced as she leaned backward across his lap. Her breast was in violent commotion, as if sadness, joy, and the potent sake were mingling and reacting within her. The lieutenant looked down into his wife's face. It was the last face he would see in this world, the last face he would see of his wife. The lieutenant scrutinized the face minutely, with the eyes of a traveller bidding farewell to splendid vistas which he will never revisit. It was a face he could not tire of looking at – the features regular yet not cold, the lips tightly closed with a soft strength. The lieutenant kissed those lips, unthinkingly. And suddenly, though there was not the slightest distortion of the face into the unsightliness of sobbing, he noticed that tears were welling slowly from beneath the long lashes of the closed eyes and brimming over into a glistening stream.

When, a little later, the lieutenant urged that they should move to the upstairs bedroom, his wife replied that she would follow after taking a bath. Climbing the stairs alone to the bedroom, where the air was already warmed by the gas heater, the lieutenant lay down on the bedding with arms outstretched and legs apart. Even the time at which he lay waiting for his wife to join him was no later and no earlier than usual.

He folded his hands beneath his head and gazed at the dark boards of the ceiling in the dimness beyond the range of the standard lamp. Was it death he was now waiting for? Or a wild ecstasy of the senses? The two seemed to overlap, almost as if the object of this bodily desire was death itself. But, however that might be, it was certain that never before had the lieutenant tasted such total freedom.

There was the sound of a car outside the window. He could hear the screech of its tyres skidding in the snow piled at the side of the street. The sound of its horn re-echoed from nearby walls. . . . Listening to these noises he had the feeling that this house rose like a solitary island in the ocean of a society going as restlessly about its business as ever. All around, vastly and untidily, stretched the country for which he grieved. He was to give his life for it. But would that great country, with which he was prepared to remonstrate to the extent of destroying himself, take the slightest heed of his death? He did not know; and it did not matter. His was a battlefield without glory, a battlefield where none could display deeds of valour: it was the front line of the spirit.

Reiko's footsteps sounded on the stairway. The steep stairs in this old house creaked badly. There were fond memories in that creaking, and many a time, while waiting in bed, the lieutenant had listened to its welcome sound. At the thought that he would hear it no more he listened with intense concentration, striving for every corner of every moment of this precious time to be filled with the sound of those soft footfalls on the creaking stairway. The moments seemed transformed to jewels, sparkling with inner light.

Reiko wore a Nagoya sash about the waist of her *yukata*, but as the lieutenant, reached towards it, its redness sobered by the dimness of the light, Reiko's hand moved to his assistance and the sash fell away, slithering swiftly to the floor. As she stood before him, still in her *yukata*, the lieutenant inserted his hands through the side slits beneath each sleeve, intending to embrace her as she was; but at the touch of his finger-tips upon the warm, naked flesh, and as the armpits closed gently about his hands, his whole body was suddenly aflame.

In a few moments the two lay naked before the glowing gas heater.

Neither spoke the thought, but their hearts, their bodies, and their pounding breasts blazed with the knowledge that this was the very last time. It was as if the words 'The Last Time' were spelled out, in invisible brushstrokes, across every inch of their bodies.

The lieutenant drew his wife close and kissed her vehemently. As their tongues explored each other's mouths, reaching out into the smooth, moist interior, they felt as if the still-unknown agonies of death had tempered their senses to the keenness of red-hot steel. The agonies they could not yet feel, the distant pains of death, had refined their awareness of pleasure.

'This is the last time I shall see your body,' said the lieutenant. 'Let me look at it closely.' And, tilting the shade on the lampstand to one side, he directed the rays along the full length of Reiko's outstretched form.

Reiko lay still with her eyes closed. The light from the low lamp clearly revealed the majestic sweep of her white flesh. The lieutenant, not without a touch of egocentricity, rejoiced that he would never see this beauty crumble in death.

At his leisure, the lieutenant allowed the unforgettable spectacle to engrave itself upon his mind. With one hand he fondled the hair, with the other he softly stroked the magnificent face, implanting kisses here and there where his eyes lingered. The quiet coldness of the high, tapering forehead, the closed eyes with their long lashes beneath faintly etched brows, the set of the finely shaped nose, the gleam of teeth glimpsed between full, regular lips, the soft cheeks and the small, wise chin ... these things conjured up in the lieutenant's mind the vision of a truly radiant death face, and again and again he pressed his lips tight against the white throat – where Reiko's own hand was soon to strike – and the throat reddened faintly beneath his kisses. Returning to the mouth he laid his lips against it with the gentlest of pressures, and moved them rhythmically over Reiko's with the light rolling motion of a small boat. If he closed his eyes, the world became a rocking cradle.

Wherever the lieutenant's eyes moved his lips faithfully followed. The high, swelling breasts, surmounted by nipples like the buds of a wild cherry, hardened as the lieutenant's lips closed about them. The arms flowed smoothly downward from each side of the breast, tapering towards the wrists, yet losing nothing of their roundness or symmetry, and at their tips were those delicate fingers which had held the fan at the wedding ceremony. One by one, as the lieutenant kissed them, the fingers withdrew behind their neighbour as if in shame. . . . The natural hollow curving between the bosom and the stomach carried in its lines a suggestion not only of softness but of resilient strength, and while it gave forewarning of the rich curves spreading outward from here to the hips it had, in itself, an appearance only of restraint and proper discipline. The whiteness and richness of the stomach and hips was like milk brimming in a great bowl, and the sharply shadowed dip of the navel could have been the fresh impress of a raindrop, fallen there that very moment. Where the shadows gathered more thickly, hair clustered, gentle and sensitive, and as the agitation mounted in the now no longer passive body there hung over this region a scent like the smouldering of fragrant blossoms, growing steadily more pervasive.

At length, in a tremulous voice, Reiko spoke.

'Show me. . . . Let me look too, for the last time.'

Never before had he heard from his wife's lips so strong and unequivocal a request. It was as if something which her modesty had wished to keep hidden to the end had suddenly burst its bonds of restraint. The lieutenant obediently lay back and surrendered himself to his wife. Lithely she raised her white, trembling body and – burning with an innocent desire to return to her husband what he had done for her – placed two white fingers on the lieutenant's eyes, which gazed fixedly up at her, and gently stroked them shut.

Suddenly overwhelmed by tenderness, her cheeks flushed by a dizzying uprush of emotion, Reiko threw her arms about the lieutenant's close-cropped head. The bristly hairs rubbed painfully against her breast, the prominent nose was cold as it dug into her flesh, and his breath was hot. Relaxing her embrace, she gazed down at her husband's masculine face. The severe brows, the closed eyes, the splendid bridge of the nose, the shapely lips drawn firmly together . . . the blue, clean-shaven cheeks reflecting the light and gleaming smoothly. Reiko kissed each of these. She kissed the broad nape of the neck, the strong, erect shoulders, the powerful chest with its twin circles like shields and its russet nipples. In the armpits, deeply shadowed by the ample flesh of the shoulders and chest, a sweet and melancholy odour emanated from the growth of hair, and in the sweetness of this odour was contained, somehow, the essence of young death. The lieutenant's naked skin glowed like a field of barley, and everywhere the muscles showed in sharp relief, converging on the lower abdomen about the small, unassuming navel. Gazing at the youthful, firm stomach, modestly covered by a vigorous growth of hair, Reiko thought of it as it was soon to be, cruelly cut by the sword, and she laid her head upon it, sobbing in pity, and bathed it with kisses.

At the touch of his wife's tears upon his stomach the lieutenant felt ready to endure with courage the cruellest agonies of his suicide.

What ecstasies they experienced after these tender exchanges may well be imagined. The lieutenant raised himself and enfolded his wife in a powerful embrace, her body now limp with exhaustion after her grief and tears. Passionately they held their faces close, rubbing cheek against cheek. Reiko's body was trembling. Their breasts, moist with sweat, were tightly joined, and every inch of the young and beautiful bodies had become so much one with the other that it seemed impossible there should ever again be a separation. Reiko cried out. From the heights they plunged into the abyss, and from the abyss they took wing and soared once more to dizzying heights. The lieutenant panted like the regimental standard-bearer on a route march. . . . As one cycle ended, almost immediately a new wave of passion would be generated, and together – with no trace of fatigue – they would climb again in a single breathless movement to the very summit.

3

When the lieutenant at last turned away, it was not from weariness. For one thing, he was anxious not to undermine the considerable strength he would need in carrying out his suicide. For another, he would have been sorry to mar the sweetness of these last memories by over-indulgence.

Since the lieutenant had clearly desisted, Reiko too, with her usual compliance, followed his example. The two lay naked on their backs, with fingers interlaced, staring fixedly at the dark ceiling. The room was warm from the heater, and even when the sweat had ceased to pour from their bodies they felt no cold. Outside, in the hushed night, the sounds of passing traffic had ceased. Even the noises of the trains and tramcars around Yotsuya station did not penetrate this far. After echoing through the region bounded by the moat, they were lost in the heavily wooded park fronting the broad driveway before Akasaka Palace. It was hard to believe in the tension gripping this whole quarter, where the two factions of the bitterly divided Imperial Army now confronted each other, poised for battle.

Savouring the warmth glowing within themselves, they lay still and recalled the ecstasies they had just known. Each moment of the experience was relived. They remembered the taste of kisses which had never wearied, the touch of naked flesh, episode after episode of dizzying bliss. But already, from the dark boards of the ceiling, the face of death was peering down. These joys had been final, and their bodies would never know them again. Not that joy of this intensity – and the same thought had occurred to them both – was ever likely to be re-experienced, even if they should live on to old age.

The feel of their fingers intertwined – this too would soon be lost. Even the wood-grain patterns they now gazed at on the dark ceiling boards would be taken from them. They could feel death edging in, nearer and nearer. There could be no hesitation now. They must have the courage to reach out to death themselves, and to seize it.

'Well, let's make our preparations,' said the lieutenant. The note of determination in the words was unmistakable, but at the same time Reiko had never heard her husband's voice so warm and tender.

After they had risen, a variety of tasks awaited them.

The lieutenant, who had never once before helped with the bedding, now cheerfully slid back the door of the closet, lifted the mattress across the room by himself, and stowed it away inside.

Reiko turned off the gas heater and put away the lamp standard. During the lieutenant's absence she had arranged this room carefully, sweeping and dusting it to a fresh cleanness, and now – if one overlooked the rosewood table drawn into one corner – the eight-mat room gave all the appearance of a reception room ready to welcome an important guest.

'We've seen some drinking here, haven't we? With Kanō and Homma and Noguchi . . .'

'Yes, they were great drinkers, all of them.'

'We'll be meeting them before long, in the other world. They'll tease us, I imagine, when they find I've brought you with me.'

Descending the stairs, the lieutenant turned to look back into this calm, clean room, now brightly illuminated by the ceiling lamp. There floated across his mind the faces of the young officers who had drunk there, and laughed, and innocently bragged. He had never dreamed then that he would one day cut open his stomach in this room.

In the two rooms downstairs husband and wife busied themselves smoothly and serenely with their respective preparations. The lieutenant went to the toilet, and then to the bathroom to wash. Meanwhile Reiko folded away her husband's padded robe, placed his uniform tunic, his trousers, and a newly cut bleached loincloth in the bathroom, and set out sheets of paper on the living-room table for the farewell notes. Then she removed the lid from the writing-box and began rubbing ink from the ink tablet. She had already decided upon the wording of her own note.

Reiko's fingers pressed hard upon the cold gilt letters of the ink tablet, and the water in the shallow well at once darkened, as if a black cloud had spread across it. She stopped thinking that this repeated action, this pressure from her fingers, this rise and fall of faint sound, was all and solely for death. It was a routine domestic task, a simple paring away of time until death should finally stand before her. But somehow, in the increasingly smooth motion of the tablet rubbing on the stone, and in the scent from the thickening ink, there was unspeakable darkness.

Neat in his uniform, which he now wore next to his skin, the lieutenant emerged from the bathroom. Without a word he seated himself at the table, bolt upright, took a brush in his hand, and stared undecidedly at the paper before him.

Reiko took a white silk kimono with her and entered the bathroom. When she reappeared in the living-room, clad in the white kimono and with her face lightly made up, the farewell note lay completed on the table beneath the lamp. The thick black brushstrokes said simply:

'Long Live the Imperial Forces – Army Lieutenant Takeyama Shinji.'

While Reiko sat opposite him writing her own note, the lieutenant gazed in silence, intensely serious, at the controlled movement of his wife's pale fingers as they manipulated the brush.

With their respective notes in their hands – the lieutenant's sword strapped to his side, Reiko's small dagger thrust into the sash of her white kimono – the two of them stood before the god shelf and silently prayed. Then they put out all the downstairs lights. As he mounted the stairs the lieutenant turned his head and gazed back at the striking, white-clad figure of his wife, climbing behind him, with lowered eyes, from the darkness beneath.

The farewell notes were laid side by side in the alcove of the upstairs room. They wondered whether they ought not to remove the hanging scroll, but since it had been written by their go-between, Lieutenant General Ozeki, and consisted, moreover, of two Chinese characters signifying 'Sincerity', they left it where it was. Even if it were to become stained with splashes of blood, they felt that the lieutenant general would understand.

The lieutenant, sitting erect with his back to the alcove, laid his sword on the floor before him.

Reiko sat facing him, a mat's width away. With the rest of her so severely white the touch of rouge on her lips seemed remarkably seductive.

Across the dividing mat they gazed intently into each other's eyes. The lieutenant's sword lay before his knees. Seeing it, Reiko recalled their first night and was overwhelmed with sadness. The lieutenant spoke, in a hoarse voice:

'As I have no second to help me I shall cut deep. It may look unpleasant, but please do not panic. Death of any sort is a fearful thing to watch. You must not be discouraged by what you see. Is that all right?'

'Yes.'

Reiko nodded deeply.

Looking at the slender white figure of his wife the lieutenant experienced a bizarre excitement. What he was about to perform was an act in his public capacity as a soldier, something he had never previously shown his wife. It called for a resolution equal to the courage to enter battle; it was a death of no less degree and quality than death in the front line. It was his conduct on the battlefield that he was now to display.

Momentarily the thought led the lieutenant to a strange fantasy. A lonely death on the battlefield, a death beneath the eyes of his beautiful wife . . . in the sensation that he was now to die in these two dimensions, realizing an impossible union of them both, there was sweetness beyond words. This must be the very pinnacle of good fortune, he thought. To have every moment of his death observed by those beautiful eyes it was like being borne to death on a gentle, fragrant breeze. There was some special favour here. He did not understand precisely what it was, but it was a domain unknown to others: a dispensation granted to no one else had been permitted to himself. In the radiant, bridelike figure of his white-robed wife the lieutenant seemed to see a vision of all those things he had loved and for which he was to lay down his life – the Imperial Household, the Nation, the Army Flag. All these, no less than the wife who sat before him, were presences observing him closely with clear and never-faltering eyes.

Reiko too was gazing intently at her husband, so soon to die, and she thought that never in this world had she seen anything so beautiful. The lieutenant always looked well in uniform, but now, as he contemplated death with severe brows and firmly closed lips, he revealed what was perhaps masculine beauty at its most superb.

'It's time to go,' the lieutenant said at last.

Reiko bent her body low to the mat in a deep bow. She could not raise her face. She did not wish to spoil her make-up with tears, but the tears could not be held back.

When at length she looked up she saw hazily through the tears that her husband had wound a white bandage round the blade of his now unsheathed sword, leaving five or six inches of naked steel showing at the point.

Resting the sword in its cloth wrapping on the mat before him, the lieutenant rose from his knees, resettled himself cross-legged, and unfastened the hooks of his uniform collar. His eyes no longer saw his wife. Slowly, one by one, he undid the flat brass buttons. The dusky brown chest was revealed, and then the stomach. He unclasped his belt and undid the buttons of his trousers. The pure whiteness of the thickly coiled loincloth showed itself. The lieutenant pushed the cloth down with both hands, further to ease his stomach, and then reached for the white-bandaged blade of his sword. With his left hand he massaged his abdomen, glancing downward as he did so.

To reassure himself on the sharpness of his sword's cutting edge the lieutenant folded back the left trouser flap, exposing a little of his thigh, and lightly drew the blade across the skin. Blood welled up in the wound at once, and several streaks of red trickled downward, glistening in the strong light.

It was the first time Reiko had ever seen her husband's blood, and she felt a violent throbbing in her chest. She looked at her husband's face. The lieutenant was looking at the blood with calm appraisal. For a moment – though thinking at the same time that it was hollow comfort – Reiko experienced a sense of relief.

The lieutenant's eyes fixed his wife with an intense, hawk-like stare. Moving the sword around to his front, he raised himself slightly on his hips and let the upper half of his body lean over the sword point. That he was mustering his whole strength was apparent from the angry tension of the uniform at his shoulders. The lieutenant aimed to strike deep into the left of his stomach. His sharp cry pierced the silence of the room.

Despite the effort he had himself put into the blow, the lieutenant had the impression that someone else had struck the side of his stomach agonizingly with a thick rod of iron. For a second or so his head reeled and he had no idea what had happened. The five or six inches of naked point had vanished completely into his flesh, and the white bandage, gripped in his clenched fist, pressed directly against his stomach.

He returned to consciousness. The blade had certainly pierced the wall of the stomach, he thought. His breathing was difficult, his chest thumped violently, and in some far deep region, which he could hardly believe was a part of himself, a fearful and excruciating pain came welling up as if the ground had split open to disgorge a boiling stream of molten rock. The pain came suddenly nearer, with terrifying speed. The lieutenant bit his lower lip and stifled an instinctive moan.

Was this *seppuku*? – he was thinking. It was a sensation of utter chaos, as if the sky had fallen on his head and the world was reeling drunkenly. His will-power and courage, which had seemed so robust before he made the incision, had now dwindled to something like a single hairlike thread of steel, and he was assailed by the uneasy feeling that he must advance along this thread, clinging to it with desperation. His clenched fist had grown moist. Looking down, he saw that both his hand and the cloth about the blade were drenched in blood. His loincloth too was dyed a deep red. It struck him as incredible that, amidst this terrible agony, things which could be seen could still be seen, and existing things existed still.

The moment the lieutenant thrust the sword into his left side and she saw the deathly pallor fall across his face, like an abruptly lowered curtain, Reiko had to struggle to prevent herself from rushing to his side. Whatever happened, she must watch. She must be a witness. That was the duty her husband had laid upon her. Opposite her, a mat's space away, she could clearly see her husband biting his lip to stifle the pain. The pain was there, with absolute certainty, before her eyes. And Reiko had no means of rescuing him from it.

The sweat glistened on her husband's forehead. The lieutenant closed his eyes, and then opened them again, as if experimenting. The eyes had lost their lustre, and seemed innocent and empty like the eyes of a small animal.

The agony before Reiko's eyes burned as strong as the summer sun, utterly remote from the grief which seemed to be tearing herself apart within. The pain grew steadily in stature, stretching upward. Reiko felt that her husband had already become a man in a separate world, a man whose whole being had been resolved into pain, a prisoner in a cage of pain where no hand could reach out to him. But Reiko felt no pain at all. Her grief was not pain. As she thought about this, Reiko began to feel as if someone had raised a cruel wall of glass high between herself and her husband.

Ever since her marriage her husband's existence had been her own existence, and every breath of his had been a breath drawn by herself. But now, while her husband's existence in pain was a vivid reality, Reiko could find in this grief of hers no certain proof at all of her own existence.

With only his right hand on the sword the lieutenant began to cut sideways across his stomach. But as the blade became entangled with the entrails it was pushed constantly outward by their soft resilience; and the lieutenant realized that it would be necessary, as he cut, to use both hands to keep the point pressed deep into his stomach. He pulled the blade across. It did not cut as easily as he had expected. He directed the strength of his whole body into his right hand and pulled again. There was a cut of three or four inches.

The pain spread slowly outward from the inner depths until the whole stomach reverberated. It was like the wild clanging of a bell. Or like a thousand bells which jangled simultaneously at every breath he breathed and every throb of his pulse, rocking his whole being. The lieutenant could no longer stop himself from moaning. But by now the blade had cut its way through to below the navel, and when he noticed this he felt a sense of satisfaction, and a renewal of courage.

The volume of blood had steadily increased, and now it spurted from the wound as if propelled by the beat of the pulse. The mat before the lieutenant was drenched red with spattered blood, and more blood overflowed on to it from pools which gathered in the folds of the lieutenant's khaki trousers. A spot, like a bird, came flying across to Reiko and settled on the lap of her white silk kimono.

By the time the lieutenant had at last drawn the sword across to the right side of his stomach, the blade was already cutting shallow and had revealed its naked tip, slippery with blood and grease. But, suddenly stricken by a fit of vomiting, the lieutenant cried out hoarsely. The vomiting made the fierce pain fiercer still, and the stomach, which had thus far remained firm and compact, now abruptly heaved, opening wide its wound, and the entrails burst through, as if the wound too were vomiting. Seemingly ignorant of their master's suffering, the entrails gave an impression of robust health and almost disagreeable vitality as they slipped smoothly out and spilled over into the crotch. The lieutenant's head dropped, his shoulders heaved, his eyes opened to narrow slits, and a thin trickle of saliva dribbled from his mouth. The gold markings on his epaulettes caught the light and glinted.

Blood was scattered everywhere. The lieutenant was soaked in it to his knees, and he sat now in a crumpled and listless posture, one hand on the floor. A raw smell filled the room. The lieutenant, his head drooping, retched repeatedly, and the movement showed vividly in his shoulders. The blade of the sword, now pushed back by the entrails and exposed to its tip, was still in the lieutenant's right hand.

It would be difficult to imagine a more heroic sight than that of the lieutenant at this moment, as he mustered his strength and flung back his head. The movement was performed with sudden violence, and the back of his head struck with a sharp crack against the alcove pillar. Reiko had been sitting until now with her face lowered, gazing in fascination at the tide of blood advancing towards her knees, but the sound took her by surprise and she looked up.

The lieutenant's face was not the face of a living man. The eyes were hollow, the skin parched, the once so lustrous cheeks and lips the colour of dried mud. The right hand alone was moving. Laboriously gripping the sword, it hovered shakily in the air like the hand of a marionette and strove to direct the point at the base of the lieutenant's throat. Reiko watched her husband make this last, most heart-rending, futile exertion. Glistening with blood and grease, the point was thrust at the throat again and again. And each time it missed its aim. The strength to guide it was no longer there. The straying point struck the collar and the collar badges. Although its hooks had been unfastened, the stiff military collar had closed together again and was protecting the throat.

Reiko could bear the sight no longer. She tried to go to her husband's help, but she could not stand. She moved through the blood on her knees, and her white skirts grew deep red. Moving to the rear of her husband, she helped no more than by loosening the collar. The quivering blade at last contacted the naked flesh of the throat. At that moment Reiko's impression was that she herself had propelled her husband forward; but that was not the case. It was a movement planned by the lieutenant himself, his last exertion of strength. Abruptly he threw his body at the blade, and the blade pierced his neck, emerging at the nape. There was a tremendous spurt of blood and the lieutenant lay still, cold blue-tinged steel protruding from his neck at the back.

4

Slowly, her socks slippery with blood, Reiko descended the stairway. The upstairs room was now completely still.

Switching on the ground-floor lights, she turned off the gas-jet and the main gas tap and poured water over the smouldering, half-burned charcoal in the brazier. She stood before the upright mirror in the four-and-a-half-mat room and held up her skirts. The bloodstains made it seem as if a bold, vivid pattern was printed across the lower half of her white kimono. When she sat down before the mirror, she was conscious of the dampness and coldness of her husband's blood in the region of her thighs, and she shivered. Then, for a long while, she lingered over her toilet preparations. She applied the rouge generously to her cheeks, and her lips too she painted heavily. This was no longer make-up to please her husband. It was make-up for the world which she would leave behind, and there was a touch of the magnificent and the spectacular in her brushwork. When she rose, the mat before the mirror was wet with blood. Reiko was not concerned about this.

Returning from the toilet, Reiko stood finally on the cement floor of the porchway. When her husband had bolted the door here last night it had been in preparation for death. For a while she stood immersed in the consideration of a simple problem. Should she now leave the bolt drawn? If she were to lock the door, it could be that the neighbours might not notice their suicide for several days. Reiko did not relish the thought of their two corpses putrefying before discovery. After all, it seemed, it would be best to leave it open. . . . She released the bolt, and also drew open the frosted-glass door a fraction. . . . At once a chill wind blew in. There was no sign of anyone in the midnight streets, and stars glittered ice-cold through the trees in the large house opposite.

Leaving the door as it was, Reiko mounted the stairs. She had walked here and there for some time and her socks were no longer slippery. About half-way up, her nostrils were already assailed by a peculiar smell.

The lieutenant was lying on his face in a sea of blood. The point protruding from his neck seemed to have grown even more prominent than before. Reiko walked heedlessly across the blood. Sitting besides the lieutenant's corpse, she stared intently at the face, which lay on one cheek on the mat. The eyes were opened wide, as if the lieutenant's attention had been attracted by something. She raised the head, folding it in her sleeve, wiped the blood from the lips, and bestowed a last kiss.

Then she rose and took from the closet a new white blanket and a waist cord. To prevent any derangement of her skirts, she wrapped the blanket about her waist and bound it there firmly with the cord.

Reiko sat herself on a spot about one foot distant from the lieutenant's body. Drawing the dagger from her sash, she examined its dully gleaming blade intently, and held it to her tongue. The taste of the polished steel was slightly sweet.

Reiko did not linger. When she thought how the pain which had previously opened such a gulf between herself and her dying husband was now to become a part of her own experience, she saw before her only the joy of herself entering a realm her husband had already made his own. In her husband's agonized face there had been something inexplicable which she was seeing for the first time. Now she would solve that riddle. Reiko sensed that at last she too would be able to taste the true bitterness and sweetness of that great moral principle in which her husband believed. What had until now been tasted only faintly through her husband's example she was about to savour directly with her own tongue.

Reiko rested the point of the blade against the base of her throat. She thrust hard. The wound was only shallow. Her head blazed, and her hands shook uncontrollably. She gave the blade a strong pull sideways. A warm substance flooded into her mouth, and everything before her eyes reddened, in a vision of spouting blood. She gathered her strength and plunged the point of the blade deep into her throat.

Translated by Geoffrey W. Sargent

Dōjōji

Characters

Kiyoko, *a dancer*
Dealer in Antiques
Superintendent of Apartment House
Men A, C, E
Women B, D

A room in what is in fact a secondhand furniture shop, though it is so filled with antiques – both Oriental and Occidental – that it might more properly be called a museum. In the centre, a little to stage left, an immense wardrobe hulks like a ghostly apparition – big enough, one might suppose, to swallow up the whole world. The outline of a bell is carved into the huge doors, and the wardrobe itself is covered with a profusion of baroque ornamentation. Not surprisingly, the other objects in the shop are quite eclipsed by such a prodigy; they may therefore be represented merely on a backdrop.

Five chairs are placed here and there on the stage. On each sits a prosperous-looking man or woman who is listening to the DEALER *describing the wardrobe before which he stands. These five distinguished clients have come to today's auction by invitation.*

DEALER: Would you kindly look this way? We have here an item absolutely unique in East or West, in ancient or modern times, a wardrobe which transcends all normal practical use. The objects which we offer here are without exception the creations of artists who despised base considerations of utility, and their significance comes from the fact that you, ladies and gentlemen, are able to turn them to practical use. The average person is satisfied with standardized merchandise. When he buys a piece of furniture, it is just the same as when he buys a pet – he invariably chooses one which suits his social position and which is perfectly familiar. This accounts for his taste in mass-produced tables and chairs, in television sets, and in electric washing machines.

You ladies and gentlemen, on the other hand, with your refined sensibilities and your aloofness from popular tastes, would not, I am sure, deign even to glance at a household pet – I daresay you would infinitely prefer to buy a wild beast. You have before you an article utterly beyond the average man's comprehension, an article which, were it not for the elegance and boldness of your tastes, could never be appreciated. [*He points at the wardrobe.*] Here, indeed, is the wild beast to which I referred.

MAN A: What's it made of?

DEALER: Pardon me!

MAN A: What kind of wood is it?

DEALER [*knocking on the wardrobe*]: The genuine and indisputable – you can tell by the sound – the genuine and indisputable mahogany – Please excuse the abruptness of the question, but just for my information, could you kindly tell me approximately how many suits of clothes you own?

MAN A: One hundred and fifty.

WOMAN B: Three hundred ... oh, perhaps three hundred and seventy.

MAN C: I've never counted.

WOMAN D: Three hundred and seventy-one.

MAN E: Seven hundred.

DEALER: It doesn't surprise me. I am not surprised to hear even such figures. But whether you have seven hundred suits or a thousand, they'll all fit into this wardrobe without the least difficulty. If you will kindly look inside [*he himself glances in briefly*], you will observe the amazing capacity. It's not quite a tennis court, but it's certainly large enough for knocking-up exercises. It is lined on all four sides with mirrors, and there is also an electric light inside. You may go in, select the costume you desire, and attire yourself, all without leaving the wardrobe. Step up please, don't be bashful. Yes, look right in. Everyone will have a turn, no pushing, please. One line, if you please.

[*The five clients form a line and one after another look inside the wardrobe.*]

MAN A [*nothing surprises him; turns to proprietor after looking*]: Whose is it?

DEALER: Pardon me!

MAN A: I mean, where did you get it?

DEALER: I am not at liberty to disclose more than that it comes from a certain private collection. A very important family, before the war a family of the kind you could count on the fingers of one hand. Of late it has rather – we all know many such examples, don't we? – yes, there are quite a few such cases, and it's certainly a great shame – but this family has gone down a bit in the world, and they've been obliged . . .

MAN A: I see. You needn't say any more. [*He returns to his seat.*]

WOMAN B [*looks inside and shrieks*]: Good heavens! You could put a double bed inside!

DEALER: Yes, you're quite right. A double bed – very aptly put.

MAN C [*looks inside*]: It looks like my family crypt. I could easily put a hundred, maybe two hundred, urns in here.

DEALER [*with an expression of distaste*]: Very amusing.

WOMAN D [*looking in*]: What's the key for?

DEALER: The key? You can lock the wardrobe from the outside or the inside, whichever you please.

WOMAN D: From the inside?

DEALER [*flustered*]: I don't know why it was made that way, but there you have it.

WOMAN D: Why should anyone want to lock it from the inside?

DEALER: Well – er . . . [*He smiles meaningfully.*] I'm sure there must be some way of making use of it. After all, it's big enough to put a bed inside.

MAN E [*looking in*]: Hmm. Surprisingly small, isn't it?

DEALER: Small?

MAN E: Surprisingly.

DEALER: Do you think so, sir? Everyone has his own way of looking at things, I'm sure. [*They settle themselves in their chairs again with a great rustling and shuffling.*] Well, then, ladies and gentlemen, now you've seen it. I hate to hurry you, but I propose to offer it now at auction. What am I bid for it? Speak up please.

Anyone, please. [*They are all silent.*] Come, come, does no one wish to bid for it?

MAN A: Fifty thousand yen.

DEALER: I have fifty thousand yen.

WOMAN B: Fifty-one thousand yen.

DEALER: The lady bids fifty-one thousand yen.

MAN C: One hundred thousand yen.

DEALER: One hundred thousand yen here.

WOMAN D: One hundred and fifty thousand yen.

DEALER: I'm bid one hundred and fifty thousand yen.

MAN E: One hundred and eighty thousand yen.

DEALER: Yes, one hundred and eighty thousand yen.

VOICE [*a woman's voice from stage right*]: Three thousand yen.

[*They all turn round.*]

MAN A: Three thousand five hundred yen.

DEALER: The bid is three thousand five hundred yen. Eh? What was that? I'm afraid you must have heard wrong, sir. The bid stood at one hundred and eighty thousand yen. The last bid was one hundred and eighty thousand yen.

MAN A: All right. One hundred and ninety thousand yen.

DEALER: I have one hundred and ninety thousand yen.

MAN C: Two hundred and fifty thousand yen.

DEALER: Two hundred and fifty thousand yen is the bid.

MAN E: Three hundred thousand yen.

DEALER: Three hundred thousand yen it is.

WOMAN B: Three hundred and fifty thousand yen.

WOMAN D: Three hundred and sixty thousand yen.

WOMAN B [*annoyed*]: Really! Five hundred thousand yen.

WOMAN D: Five hundred and ten thousand yen.

WOMAN B: Again! One million yen.

WOMAN D: One million ten thousand yen.

WOMAN B: This is going too far. Two million yen.

WOMAN D: Two million ten thousand yen.

WOMAN B: If that isn't impudence! Three million yen.

WOMAN D: Three million ten thousand yen.

WOMAN B: Ohhh –

VOICE [*the same woman's voice, from stage right*]: Three thousand yen. Three thousand yen.

[*They all look to right with various exclamations of surprise. A beautiful young woman quietly enters. She is* KIYOKO, *a dancer.*]

DEALER: Who are you? I've had quite enough of your peculiar sense of humour. Of all times! Really, you're carrying foolishness a bit too far. Who are you anyway?

KIYOKO: You'd like to know my name? I'm Kiyoko. I'm a dancer.

[MEN A, C, *and* E *look at her with considerable interest.*]

DEALER: A dancer! I don't remember having asked you here. This sale is restricted to invited customers. Didn't you see the sign at the door 'By Invitation Only'?

KIYOKO: The sign was twisted over by the wind. Anyway, I have qualifications to be here, even if I'm not invited.

DEALER: Just listen to her talk! – Come, leave at once. I'll let you off this time without taking you to the police.

MAN A: Why not let her stay? She must have some good reason for being here. Don't shout at her that way.

DEALER: I know, sir, but . . .

MAN A: What's your business here, young lady?

KIYOKO: I'm not a young lady. I'm only a dancer.

MAN C: That's fine. A dancer, she says.

MAN E: A dancer – an admirable profession. Bringing comfort to to us all, a blessing money can't buy.

WOMAN B: What do you mean by offering three thousand yen?

WOMAN D: Three thousand and one yen.

WOMAN B: Of all the infuriating people! [*To* KIYOKO, *in honeyed tones*] You said your name was Kiyoko, didn't you? What did you mean by offering three thousand yen? Do come here and talk to us.

KIYOKO: Three thousand yen . . . [*She goes to the centre.*] Three thousand yen is all that wardrobe is worth.

DEALER [*in consternation*]: See here. Any more foolish talk like that, and it's off to the police with you.

MAN A [*to* DEALER]: Listen quietly to what she has to say.

[DEALER *is silent.*]

KIYOKO: Once you've heard the history of this enormous, strange wardrobe, I don't think any of you will want to buy it.

MAN C: It has a history?

DEALER [*quickly wrapping some money in a piece of paper*]: Here, take this and leave. We've had quite enough. Come. At once.

MAN A: Let her talk. If you don't let her talk we'll know that you're also familiar with its history. Are you trying to pass off a defective article?

KIYOKO [*spurning the money*]: I'll tell you then. This wardrobe belonged to the Sakurayama family. [*General stir.*] Mrs Sakurayama used to hide her young lover inside the wardrobe. The lover's name was Yasushi. One day her jealous husband – he was a terrifying man – heard a noise inside the wardrobe. He took out his pistol and without a word fired from the outside. He fired and fired until the horrible screams finally died away and the blood came gushing through the crack under the wardrobe door. Look. [*She points at the door.*] You can't see very well because of the carving, but this is where the bullet holes were. Here and here, look. They've repaired the holes very cleverly and filled them in with wood of the same colour, but you can still see them. . . . They've washed away every trace of the blood from inside the door, they've planed the door down and then repainted it. . . . You've all read about what happened in the newspapers, haven't you? [*They are absolutely quiet.*] Do you still want to buy it for all that money? No, I'm sure you wouldn't want the wardrobe, even if it were offered to you as a gift. Three thousand yen is a good price. Even at three thousand yen there can't be many people besides myself who'd buy it.

WOMAN B: Ugh! How gruesome! I really appreciate your having told us. If you hadn't, I'd have spent a fortune acquiring a horrible jinx – Did you say your name was Hisako?

KIYOKO: It's Ki-yo-ko.

WOMAN B: That's right. Hisako's my daughter's name. Kiyoko, thank you very much indeed. Under the circumstances the best thing to do is to leave as quickly as possible. I wonder if my chauffeur is still waiting. I told him to. [*She suddenly notices that* WOMAN D *has already disappeared.*] Oh, can you imagine anyone being so ill-mannered? Leaving that way without a word. She's always trying to outdo me, even when it comes to leaving a place. Unspeakable creature! [*So saying, she exits to right.*]

[MEN A, C *and* E *variously approach* KIYOKO *and offer their cards.*]

MAN A: You've saved me a bit of money. Thanks very much. I'd like to take you to dinner – nothing special, of course – just to show my appreciation.

MAN C: Miss, I'll take you to a really good French restaurant.

MAN E: How about a dance? Eh? After dinner together.

KIYOKO: Thank you all, but I have something to discuss with the proprietor.

MAN A [*with the brusque movements of a man of decision, he takes some money from his wallet and hands it to the* DEALER]: Understand? You're not to start any trouble. You'll listen quietly to what this young lady has to say, like a father. No more nonsense about the police. Understand? [*He takes a pencil from his pocket. To* KIYOKO] Young lady. Let me know immediately if this man uses rough language or starts threatening to take you to the police. Would you show me those cards you were just given? [KIYOKO *holds up the three cards.*] Here we are. [*He takes one of the cards.*] This is mine. I'll put a mark on it so you won't mistake it. [*He makes a mark with his pencil.*] I'll be waiting for your call when you've finished your business. You can get me at the telephone number on the card for another two hours. [*He returns the card.* C *and* E, *dismayed at this turn of events, glower.*] You'll be sure to come, won't you? I'm hoping very much I can take you to dinner, to show my appreciation.

KIYOKO: Supposing I call you . . .

MAN A: Yes?

KIYOKO: Supposing I call you . . . would you still want to see me even if my face were completely changed?

MAN A: Very witty, very witty, I'm sure, young lady. I'm afraid I don't quite get the point, but still . . .

KIYOKO: Even if I turned into a horrible old witch?

MAN A: Every woman has many different faces. It takes more than that to surprise a man at my age. Well, I'll be seeing you later.

[A *saunters out cheerfully.* C *and* E *follow reluctantly.*]

DEALER: Quite the little terror, aren't you? [KIYOKO *turns round and starts after* A. DEALER, *alarmed, stops her.*] Don't get so excited. I'm a little on edge myself. . . . You said you were a dancer. [*To himself*] Dancer, indeed. I can imagine the kind of dancer she is.

KIYOKO: Please listen to what I have to say without interrupting.

DEALER [*sitting on one of the chairs*]: Very well. I'm listening. I won't interrupt. But to think that someone so young, with such a beautiful, sweet face –

KIYOKO: Yes. That's what I want to talk to you about – my beautiful, sweet face.

DEALER [*to himself*]: How cheeky they are, the girls these days!

KIYOKO: Yasushi was my lover.

DEALER: The young man who got killed inside the wardrobe?

KIYOKO: Yes. He was my lover, but he jilted me and became the lover of Mrs Sakurayama, a woman ten years older than himself. He – yes, that's right – he was the kind of man who always prefers to be loved.

DEALER: That was too bad for you.

KIYOKO: I thought you said you weren't going to interrupt – Perhaps, I can't be sure, it was my love that drove him away. Yes, that may have been it. Rather than a happy, easy-going, open love affair, he preferred uneasiness, secrecy, fear – that sort of thing. He was such a handsome boy. When the two of us went out walking together, everybody would say what a perfectly matched couple we made. When we walked together, the blue sky, the woods in the park, the birds – they all were glad to welcome us. The blue sky and the night sky filled with stars belonged to us, you might say. And yet, he chose the inside of a wardrobe.

DEALER: This wardrobe's so big. Maybe there was a sky inside it with stars, and a moon coming up from one corner and sinking in another.

KIYOKO: Yes, he slept inside, woke up inside, and sometimes he ate his meals inside. In this strange, windowless room, this room where the wind never blew and trees never rustled, a room like a coffin, a tomb where he was buried alive. He chose to live in a coffin even before he was killed. A room of pleasure and of death, enveloped in the lingering scent of the woman's perfume, and the odour of his own body.... His body smelled of jasmine.

DEALER [*gradually warming to the description*]: Buried, not among flowers, but among her racks on racks of clothes.

KIYOKO: Lace flowers, satin flowers, cold, dead, strong-scented flowers.

DEALER [*to himself*]: It was damned clever of him. I'd like to die that way myself.

KIYOKO: He died exactly as he hoped. I understand that quite clearly now. And yet, why did he do it? What did he want to run away from? What was he trying so desperately to escape that he preferred to die?

DEALER: I'm afraid I'm not much help answering that.

KIYOKO: I'm sure what he wanted to escape was me. [*They are both silent.*] Tell me, what could have made him do it? Run away from me, from such a beautiful, sweet face. Perhaps his own beauty gave him all the beauty he could stand.

DEALER: You've got nothing to complain about. Some women spend their whole lives furious at their own ugly faces. Any number yearn for lost youth. You've got beauty and youth, and still you complain. That's asking too much.

KIYOKO: Nobody else ever ran away from my youth and beauty. He spurned the only two treasures I own.

DEALER: Yasushi isn't the only man, you know. There must've been something abnormal about his tastes, anyway. Take a man like myself, a man whose tastes are completely healthy . . . [*He extends one hand towards her.*]

KIYOKO [*striking his hand sharply*]: Stop it. Desire on any other man's face except his turns my stomach. It's as if I saw a toad. . . . Look at me carefully. I've become old, haven't I?

DEALER: Don't make me laugh. With your youth –

KIYOKO: But I'm ugly.

DEALER: If you're ugly, then there aren't any beautiful women left in the world.

KIYOKO: You've failed on both questions. If you had said that I was old and ugly, who knows, I might have given myself to you.

DEALER: I know a bit about the psychology of women myself. Now I'm supposed to repeat, 'Whatever can you be saying? Never, though I died for it, could I possibly utter so dreadful a lie as to say that you were old and ugly.' Am I right?

KIYOKO: How tedious you are. What is it in my face that attracts men I can't stand? I'd like to rip the skin away with my own hands – that's the one dream, the one fantasy left me now. Sometimes I wonder if he wouldn't have loved me better if my face had become hideous and repulsive.

DEALER: The crazy dreams that young, beautiful people have! I long ago became immune to such illogical dreams. Discontent, young lady, is a poison which upsets all the sane principles of the world and makes a mess of your own happiness.

KIYOKO: Discontent! You think you can sum me up with that little word! That's not the kind of world I live in. Something was missing somewhere – a cogwheel – that could have made it possible for him and myself to love each other for ever, for the machine to run smoothly. I've discovered what the missing cogwheel was. It was my face turned hideous.

DEALER: The world is full of missing cogwheels. I don't know about your machine, but it seems to me, at least as far as this globe is concerned, that the one thing that keeps it spinning smoothly is the cogwheels missing here and there.

KIYOKO: Still, if my dream were to come true . . .

DEALER: Surely he wouldn't come back to life.

KIYOKO: You're wrong. I think he might.

DEALER: You keep asking for more and more impossible things. Now you're thought up something really horrible. You're trying to deny nature.

KIYOKO: Once in a while even a pitiful old miser like yourself is capable of saying something intelligent. You're quite right. My enemy, my rival for his love, was not Mrs Sakurayama. It was nature itself, my beautiful face, the rustle of the woods embracing us, the gracefully shaped pines, the blue sky damp after a rain. Yes, every unadorned thing was the enemy of our love. Then he left me and ran off into this wardrobe, into a world painted in varnish, a world without windows, a world lit only by an electric bulb.

DEALER: I suppose that's why you have your heart set on buying the wardrobe – you want to try to find your dead lover again inside.

KIYOKO: Yes, I'll spread the word; I'll tell the history of this wardrobe to everybody who might conceivably buy it; I'll disillusion them. I must have this wardrobe and at my price, three thousand yen.

[*As she finishes these words, strange inarticulate cries, like those made by the drummers in a nō play, are heard from the left, together with sounds resembling the nō drums and flute. These accompany the dialogue in the following scene as the two dispute the price of the wardrobe, producing the effect of the rhythms of the nō.*]

DEALER: Damn it. Those crazy shouts and that pounding noise have started again in the factory. Sometimes it goes on when I have customers here, and it drives me frantic. One of these days I'll have to buy the property and get rid of that factory. The sound of production – that's what our industrialists call it. Poor fools, as long as they live, they'll never grasp the simple fact that an article only acquires value as it gradually becomes old, obsolete, and useless. They turn out their cheap gadgets as quickly as they can, and after a life haunted by poverty, they die, and that's that.

KIYOKO: I've told you again and again. I'll buy it for three thousand yen.

DEALER: Three million yen.

KIYOKO: No, no, three thousand yen.

DEALER: Two million yen.

KIYOKO [*stamping her feet to the nō rhythm*]: No, no, three thousand yen.

DEALER: One million yen.

KIYOKO: No, three thousand yen.

DEALER: Five hundred thousand yen.

KIYOKO: Three thousand yen, three thousand yen, three thousand yen.

DEALER: Four hundred thousand yen.

KIYOKO: When I say three thousand yen, I mean three thousand yen.

DEALER: Three hundred thousand yen.

KIYOKO: Make an effort, one great effort. Come down to my level, all the way down. You'll feel wonderful once you've made the plunge, all the way down to three thousand yen. Come, it takes only one word from you. Three thousand yen.

DEALER: Two hundred thousand yen.
KIYOKO: No, no, three thousand yen.
DEALER: One hundred thousand yen.
KIYOKO: No, no, three thousand yen.
DEALER: Fifty thousand yen.
KIYOKO: No, three thousand yen, three thousand yen, three thousand yen.
DEALER: Fifty thousand yen. I won't come down another penny.
KIYOKO: Three thousand yen.
DEALER: Fifty thousand yen, fifty thousand yen, fifty thousand yen.
KIYOKO [*somewhat weaker*]: Three thousand yen.
DEALER: Fifty thousand yen is my rock-bottom price. I won't come down a penny more.
KIYOKO: You're sure?
DEALER: I said fifty thousand yen and I meant fifty thousand yen.
KIYOKO [*weakening*]: I haven't got that much money.
DEALER: I'm offering it to you at the price it cost me. If you haven't got the money, it's not my fault.

[*The noise to left stops completely.*]

KIYOKO: Nothing will change your mind?
DEALER: Fifty thousand yen. That's my final offer. Fifty thousand yen.
KIYOKO: I can't afford it. I wanted to buy it and cram it into my tiny apartment, and sit inside thinking of him till I felt my face become hideous – that was my dream. But if I can't have it, that's all right. [*She slowly edges backward towards the wardrobe.*] Yes, if I can't have it, it's quite all right. It's not really necessary to take this wardrobe all the way back to my apartment in order for my jealousy and my dreams and my pains and my anguish to destroy my face. I can leave it here, without moving it . . .
DEALER: What are you doing?
KIYOKO: It's all right. The next time you see me, you'll drop dead of fright!

[KIYOKO *wheels round and slips into the wardrobe. The doors slam shut with a terrible finality. The* DEALER *frantically tries to open the doors, but he is unsuccessful.*]

DEALER: Damn it. She's locked it from the inside. [*He bangs furiously on the door. There is no answer; the inside is absolutely still.*] The shameless hussy. She caught me off my guard and now she's finally managed. . . . She wasn't satisfied with interfering with my business and making me lose a fortune. Now, on top of everything else, she's trying the ruin the wardrobe, and it's defective as it is. What have I ever done to deserve this? Damn her. There's no telling what she may be up to inside this wardrobe. [*He puts his ear to the door.*] What can she be doing in there? This certainly a black day for me. . . . I can't hear a thing. There's not a sound. It's like putting your ear to a bell. Thick iron walls absolutely silent, though sometimes they can deafen you with reverberations. It doesn't make a sound. . . . She couldn't, I'm sure, be disfiguring herself. . . . No, that was nothing but a threat, a trick to take advantage of my weakness. [*He puts his ear to the wardrobe again.*] Still, what can she be doing? It gives me the eeriest feeling. Oh – she's switched on the light. Her face is reflected in the mirrors all around her, silent, not saying a word. Ugh – there's something weird about it. . . . No, it was just a threat. [*As if he has a premonition*] It was only a threat. There's no reason to suppose she would actually go through with such a thing.

[*The* SUPERINTENDENT *of* KIYOKO'*s apartment building rushes in from right.*]

SUPERINTENDENT: Has a dancer named Kiyoko come here? A young, beautiful girl? Kiyoko's her name.

DEALER: Kiyoko? Who are you?

SUPER: I'm the superintendent of the apartment house she lives in. Are you sure she hasn't been here? If she comes –

DEALER: Steady, steady. Don't get so excited. If she comes, what then?

SUPER: Her friend tells me she just stole a bottle of sulphuric acid from his shop. He's a pharmacist.

DEALER: Sulphuric acid?

SUPER: He says she dashed out with the bottle in her hand. I've been looking everywhere for her. A man I met on the way said he saw her go into your shop.

DEALER: A-acid, you say?

SUPER: It wasn't so long ago her lover got killed. With a high-strung girl like that, there's no telling what she might do. That's what worries me. Just supposing she threw it in somebody's face.

DEALER: You think she would? [*He recoils and puts his hands to his face in fright.*] . . . No, that's not what she's planning. She's going to throw the acid in her own face.

SUPER: What?

DEALER: Yes, I mean, she'll disfigure herself. What a horrible thing to happen! That beautiful face – she's about to commit a suicide of the face.

SUPER: Why should she do such a thing?

DEALER: Don't you understand what I'm saying? [*He points at the wardrobe.*] Kiyoko is in there. She's locked it from the inside.

SUPER: That's terrible. We must get her out of there.

DEALER: The door is solid as a rock.

SUPER: All the same, we've got to do something. [*He bangs on the door.*] Kiyoko! Kiyoko!

DEALER: A face like that will turn into a witch's! What a black day this has been! [*He joins in banging on the door.*] Come out! Don't cause us any trouble. Come out!

SUPER: Kiyoko, Miss Kiyoko.

[*A horrible scream is heard from inside the wardrobe. The two men wilt abjectly. A terrible silence. The* DEALER *at length brings his hands together in an unconscious attitude of prayer. He wrings out his words.*]

DEALER: Come out. I beg you. The wardrobe is useless to me now. You can have it for three thousand yen. Three thousand yen, that's all. I'm letting you have it. Please come out. [*The door finally opens with a heart-rending screeching noise. The* DEALER *and the* SUPERINTENDENT *automatically fall back.* KIYOKO *emerges, the vial held in her hand. Her face is not in the least altered.*] Your face – nothing's happened!

SUPER: Thank heavens.

DEALER: Thank heavens, my eye. I didn't bargain on that. You're a cheat. Frightening people this way – you might've caused me apoplexy. It's no laughing matter.

KIYOKO [*calmly*]: I haven't cheated you. I really intended to throw the acid in my face.

DEALER: Then what was that scream?

KIYOKO: I switched on the light inside the wardrobe. I saw my face reflected in the mirrors all around me, and the reflections of the reflections of my face in the mirror by the mirror behind it, and these reflections reflected again. Mirrors reflecting mirrors, reflecting my profile, and the mirrors reflected again. An endless, infinite number of my faces, stretching on and on. . . . It was so cold inside the wardrobe. I was waiting, wondering if among all those faces of mine his might not suddenly appear.

DEALER [*shuddering again*]: And did it?

KIYOKO: No, it didn't. To the ends of the earth, to the ends of the sea, to the ends of the whole world, my face and only my face. I removed the cap from the bottle and I stared at my face in the mirror. I thought, Supposing my face disfigured by this acid were repeated to the ends of the earth? Suddenly I had a vision of my face after I had disfigured it, the horrible face of a witch scarred and festering.

DEALER: And then you screamed?

KIYOKO: Yes.

DEALER: That was when you lost the courage to throw the acid in your face, wasn't it?

KIYOKO: No. I came back to my senses and screwed the cap on the bottle again, not because I had lost my nerve, but because I realized that even the terrible suffering, jealousy, anger, torment, and pain I had gone through had not been enough to change a human face, that no matter what happened my face was my face.

DEALER: You see, you can't win when you fight with nature.

KIYOKO: I wasn't beaten. I became reconciled to nature.

DEALER: A convenient way of looking at it.

KIYOKO: I *have* become reconciled. [*She drops the bottle on to the floor. The* DEALER *hastens to kick it aside.*] It's spring now, isn't it? I've realized it for the first time. The seasons have meant nothing to me for such a long, long time, ever since he disappeared into this wardrobe. [*She sniffs the air around her.*] It's the height of spring. Even in this musty old shop I can smell it – where is it coming from? – a fragrance of spring earth, of plants and trees, of flowers. The cherry blossoms must be in full glory.

Clouds of blossoms, and apart from them only the pines. The strong green of the branches amidst the smoky blossoms, the outlines sharp because they've never had any dreams. The birds are singing. [*A twittering of birds is heard.*] A singing of birds passing like sunlight through the thickest walls. Even as we stand here the spring relentlessly presses in on us, with such a multitude of cherry blossoms, such a multitude of singing birds. Every last branch holds as many as it can and shuts its eyes in rapture under the delicious weight. And the wind – I can smell the fragrance of his living body in this wind. I had forgotten. It was spring!

DEALER: Will you kindly purchase the wardrobe and leave?

KIYOKO: You were saying a while ago that you'd let me have it for three thousand yen, weren't you?

DEALER: Don't be silly. That was only in case your face was disfigured. The price is still five hundred thousand yen. No, six hundred thousand.

KIYOKO: I don't want it.

DEALER: You don't?

KIYOKO: That's right. I really don't want it any more. Sell it to some foolish rich man. Don't worry. I won't make any more trouble for you.

DEALER: Thank heavens for that.

SUPER: Let's go back together to the apartment. You'll have to apologize to your friend in the pharmacy for making him worry. Then you should get a good night's sleep. You must be exhausted.

KIYOKO [*taking a card from her handbag and examining it*]: No, I have an engagement now.

SUPER: Where?

DEALER [*noticing the card* KIYOKO *holds*]: With that gentleman? Now?

KIYOKO: Yes, with that gentleman, now.

DEALER: If you go, you can be sure he'll give you quite a time.

KIYOKO: I'm not worried. Nothing can bother me, no matter what happens. Who do you suppose can wound me now?

SUPER: Spring is a dangerous season.

DEALER: You'll be ruined. Your heart'll be torn to shreds. You'll end up no longer able to feel anything.

KIYOKO: Still, nothing that happens can ever change my face.

[KIYOKO *takes a lipstick from her bag, applies it to her lips, then turning her back on the two men, who watch her blankly, she suddenly rushes off to right, fast as the wind.*]

CURTAIN

Translated by Donald Keene

Onnagata

Masuyama had been overwhelmed by Mangiku's artistry; that was how it happened that, after getting a degree in classical Japanese literature, he had chosen to join the kabuki theatre staff. He had been entranced by seeing Mangiku Sanokawa perform.

Masuyama's addiction to kabuki began when he was a high-school student. At the time, Mangiku, still a fledgling *onnagata*, was appearing in such minor roles as the ghost butterfly in *Kagami Jishi* or, at best, the waiting maid Chidori in *The Disowning of Genta*. Mangiku's acting was unassertive and orthodox; nobody suspected he would achieve his present eminence. But even in those days Masuyama sensed the icy flames given off by this actor's aloof beauty. The general public, needless to say, noticed nothing. For that matter, none of the drama critics had ever called attention to the peculiar quality of Mangiku, like shoots of flame visible through the snow, which illuminated his performances from very early in his career. Now everyone spoke as if Mangiku had been a personal discovery.

Mangiku Sanokawa was a true *onnagata*, a species seldom encountered nowadays. Unlike most contemporary *onnagata*, he was quite incapable of performing successfully in male roles. His stage presence was colourful, but with dark overtones; his every gesture was the essence of delicacy. Mangiku never expressed anything – not even strength, authority, endurance, or courage – except through the single medium open to him, feminine expression, but through this medium he could filter every variety of human emotion. That is the way of the true *onnagata* but in recent years this breed has become rare indeed. Their tonal colouring, produced by a particular, exquisitely refined musical instrument, cannot be achieved by playing a normal instrument in a minor key, nor, for that matter, is it produced by a mere slavish imitation of real women.

Yukihime, the Snow Princess, in *Kinkakuji* was one of Mangiku's most successful roles. Masuyama remembered having seen Magiku perform Yukihime ten times during a single month, but no matter how often he repeated this experience, his intoxication did not diminish. Everything symbolizing Sanokawa Mangiku may be found in this play, the elements entwined, beginning with the opening words of the narrator: 'The Golden Pavilion, the mountain retreat of Lord Yoshimitsu, Prime Minister and Monk of the Deer Park, stands three stories high, its garden graced with lovely sights: the night-lodging stone, the water trickling below the rocks, the flow of the cascade heavy with spring, the willows and cherry-trees planted together; the capital now is a vast, many-hued brocade.' The dazzling brilliance of the set, depicting cherry-trees in blossom, a waterfall, and the glittering Golden Pavilion; the drums, suggesting the dark sound of the waterfall and contributing a constant agitation to the stage; the pale, sadistic face of the lecherous Daizen Matsunaga, the rebel general; the miracle of the magic sword which shines in morning sunlight with the holy image of Fudō, but shows a dragon's form when pointed at the setting sun; the radiance of the sunset glow on the waterfall and cherry-trees; the cherry blossoms scattering down petal by petal – everything in the play exists for the sake of one woman, the beautiful, aristocratic Yukihime. There is nothing unusual about Yukihime's costume, the crimson silk robe customarily worn by young princesses. But a ghostly presence of snow befitting her name, hovers about this granddaughter of the great painter Sesshū, permeated with snow, may be sensed across the breadth of the scene; this phantom snow gives Yukihime's crimson robe its dazzling brilliance.

Masuyama loved especially the scene where the princess, bound with ropes to a cherry-tree, remembers the legend told of her grandfather, and with her toes draws in the fallen blossoms a rat, which comes to life and gnaws through the ropes binding her. It hardly needs be said that Mangiku Sanokawa did not adopt the puppetlike movements favoured by some *onnagata* in this scene. The ropes fastening him to the tree made Mangiku look lovelier than ever: all the artificial arabesques of this *onnagata* – the delicate gestures of the body, the play of the fingers, the arch of the hand – contrived though they might appear when employed for the movements of daily life, took on a strange vitality when used by Yukihime, bound to a tree. The intricate, contorted attitudes imposed by the constraint of the rope made of each instant an exquisite crisis, and the crises seemed to flow, one into the next, with the irresistible energy of successive waves.

Mangiku's performances unquestionably possessed moments of diabolic power. He used his lovely eyes so effectively that often with one flash he could create in an entire audience the illusion that the character of a scene had completely altered: when his glance embraced the stage from the *hanamichi* or the *hanamichi* from the stage, or when he darted one upward look at the bell in *Dōjōji*. In the palace scene from *Imoseyama*, Mangiku took the part of Omiwa, whose lover was stolen from her by Princess Tachibana and who has been cruelly mocked by the court ladies at the back of the stage saying, 'A groom without peer has been found for our princess! What joy for us all!' The narrator, seated at the side of the stage, declaims in powerful tones, 'Omiwa, hearing this, at once looks back.' At this moment Omiwa's character is completely transformed, and her face reveals the marks of a possessive attachment.

Masuyama felt a kind of terror every time he witnessed this moment. For an instant a diabolic shadow had swept over both the bright stage with its splendid set and beautiful costumes and over the thousands of intently watching spectators. This force clearly emanated from Mangiku's body, but at the same time transcended his flesh. Masuyama sensed in such passages something like a dark spring welling forth from this figure on the stage, this figure so imbued with softness, fragility, grace, delicacy, and feminine charms. He could not identify it, but he thought that a strange, evil presence, the final residue of the actor's fascination, a seductive evil which leads men astray and makes them drown in an instant of beauty, was the true nature of the dark spring he had detected. But one explains nothing merely by giving it a name.

Omiwa shakes her head and her hair tumbles in disarray. On the stage, to which she now returns from the *hanamichi,* Funashichi's blade is waiting to kill her.

'The house is full of music, an autumn sadness in its tone,' declaims the narrator.

There is something terrifying about the way Omiwa's feet hurry forward to her doom. The bare white feet, rushing ahead towards disaster and death, kicking the lines of her kimono askew, seem to know precisely when and where on the stage the violent emotions now urging her forward will end, and to be pressing towards the spot, rejoicing and triumphant even amidst the tortures of jealousy. The pain she reveals outwardly is backed with joy like her robe, on the outside dark and shot with gold thread, but bright with variegated silken strands within.

2

Masuyama's original decision to take employment at the theatre had been inspired by his absorption with kabuki, and especially with Mangiku; he realized also he could never escape his bondage unless he became thoroughly familiar with the world behind the scenes. He knew from what others had told him of the disenchantment to be found backstage, and he wanted to plunge into that world and taste for himself genuine disillusion.

But the disenchantment he expected somehow never came. Mangiku himself made this impossible. Mangiku faithfully maintained the injunctions of the eighteenth-century *onnagata*'s manual *Ayamegusa*, 'An *onnagata*, even in the dressing-room, must preserve the attitudes of an *onnagata*. He should be careful when he eats to face away from other people, so that they cannot see him.' Whenever Mangiku was obliged to eat in the presence of visitors, not having the time to leave his dressing-room, he would turn towards his table with a word of apology and race through his meal, so skilfully that the visitors could not even guess from behind that he was eating.

Undoubtedy, the feminine beauty displayed by Mangiku on the stage had captivated Masuyama as a man. Strangely enough, however, this spell was not broken even by close observation of Mangiku in the dressing-room. Mangiku's body, when he had removed his costume, was delicate but unmistakably a man's. Masuyama, as a matter of fact, found it rather unnerving when Mangiku, seated at his dressing-table, too scantily clad to be anything but a man, directed polite, feminine greetings towards some visitor, all the while applying a heavy coating of powder to his shoulders. If even Masuyama, long a devotee of kabuki, experienced eerie sensations on his first visits to the dressing-room, what would have been the reactions of people who dislike kabuki, because the *onnagata* make them uncomfortable, if shown such a sight?

Masuyama, however, felt relief rather than disenchantment when he saw Mangiku after a performance, naked except for the gauzy underclothes he wore in order to absorb perspiration. The sight in itself may have been grotesque, but the nature of Masuyama's fascination – its intrinsic quality, one might say – did not reside in any surface illusion, and there was accordingly no danger that such a revelation would destroy it. Even after Mangiku had disrobed, it was apparent that he was still wearing several layers of splendid costumes beneath his skin; his nakedness was a passing manifestation. Something which could account for his exquisite appearance on stage surely lay concealed within him.

Masuyama enjoyed seeing Mangiku when he returned to the dressing-room after performing a major role. The flush of the emotions of the part he had been enacting still hovered over his entire body, like sunset glow or the moon in the sky at dawn. The grand emotions of classical tragedy – emotions quite unrelated to our mundane lives – may seem to be guided, at least nominally, by historical facts – the world of disputed successions, campaigns of pacification, civil warfare, and the like – but in reality they belong to no period. They are the emotions appropriate to a stylized, grotesquely tragic world, luridly coloured in the manner of a late wood-block print. Grief that goes beyond human bounds, superhuman passions, searing love, terrifying joy, the brief cries of people trapped by circumstances too tragic for human beings to endure: such were the emotions which a moment before had lodged in Mangiku's body. It was amazing that Mangiku's slender frame could hold them and that they did not break from that delicate vessel.

Be that as it may, Mangiku a moment before had been living amidst these grandiose feelings, and he had radiated light on the stage precisely because the emotions he portrayed transcended any known to his audience. Perhaps this is true of all characters on the stage, but among present-day actors none seemed to be so honestly living stage emotions so far removed from daily life.

A passage in *Ayamegusa* states, 'Charm is the essence of the *onnagata*. But even the *onnagata* who is naturally beautiful will lose his charm if he strains to impress by his movements. If he consciously attempts to appear graceful, he will seem thoroughly corrupt instead. For this reason, unless the *onnagata* lives as a woman in his daily life, he is unlikely ever to be considered an accomplished *onnagata*. When he appears on stage, the more he concentrates on performing this or that essentially feminine action, the more masculine he will seem. I am convinced that the essential thing is how the actor behaves in real life.'

How the actor behaves in real life ... yes, Mangiku was utterly feminine in both the speech and bodily movements of his real life. If Mangiku had been more masculine in his daily life, those moments when the flush from the *onnagata* role he had been performing gradually dissolved like the high-water mark on a beach into the femininity of his daily life – itself an extension of the same make-believe – would have become an absolute division between sea and land, a bleak door shut between dream and reality. The make-believe of his daily life supported the make-believe of his stage performances. This, Masuyama was convinced, marked the true *onnagata*. An *onnagata* is the child born of the illicit union between dream and reality.

3

Once the celebrated veteran actors of the previous generation had all passed away, one on the heels of the other, Mangiku's authority backstage became absolute. His *onnagata* disciples waited on him like personal servants; indeed, the order of seniority they observed when following Mangiku on stage as maids in the wake of his princess or great lady was exactly the same they observed in the dressing-room.

Anyone pushing apart the door curtains dyed with the crest of the Sanokawa family and entering Mangiku's dressing-room was certain to be struck by a strange sensation: this charming sanctuary contained not a single man. Even members of the same troupe felt inside this room that they were in the presence of the opposite sex. Whenever Masuyama went to Mangiku's dressing-room on some errand, he had only to brush apart the door curtains to feel – even before setting foot inside – a curiously vivid, carnal sensation of being a male.

Sometimes Masuyama had gone on company business to the dressing-rooms of chorus girls backstage at revues. The rooms were filled with an almost suffocating femininity and the rough-skinned girls, sprawled about like animals in the zoo, threw bored glances at him, but he never felt so distinctly alien as in Mangiku's dressing-room; nothing in these real women made Masuyama feel particularly masculine.

The members of Mangiku's entourage exhibited no special friendliness towards Masuyama. On the contrary, he knew that they secretly gossiped about him, accusing him of being disrespectful or of giving himself airs merely because he had gone through some university. He knew too that sometimes they professed irritation at his pedantic insistence on historical facts. In the world of kabuki, academic learning unaccompanied by artistic talent is considered of no value.

Masuyama's work had its compensations too. It would happen when Mangiku had a favour to ask of someone – only, of course, when he was in good mood – that he twisted his body diagonally from his dressing-table and gave a little nod and a smile; the indescribable charm in his eyes at such moments made Masuyama feel that he wished for nothing more than to slave like a dog for this man. Mangiku himself never forgot his dignity: he never failed to maintain a certain distance, though he obviously was aware of his charms. If he had been a real woman, his whole body would have been filled with the allure in his eyes. The allure of an *onnagata* is only a momentary glimmer, but that is enough for it to exist independently and to display the eternal feminine.

Mangiku sat before the mirror after the performance of *The Castle of the Lord Protector of Hachijin*, the first item of the programme. He had removed the costume and wig he wore as Lady Hinaginu, and changed to a bathrobe, not being obliged to appear in the middle work of the programme. Masuyama, informed that Mangiku wanted to see him, had been waiting in the dressing-room for the curtain of *Hachijin*. The mirror suddenly burst into crimson flames as Mangiku returned to the room, filling the entrance with the rustle of his robes. Three disciples and dressers joined to remove what had to be removed and store it away. Those who were to leave departed, and now no one remained except for a few disciples around the hibachi in the next room. The dressing-room had all at once fallen still. From a loudspeaker in the corridor issued the sounds of stage assistants hammering as they dismantled the set for the play which had just ended. It was late November, and steam heat clouded the window-panes, bleak as in a hospital ward. White chrysanthemums bent gracefully in a cloisonné vase placed beside Mangiku's dressing-table. Mangiku, perhaps because his stage name meant literally 'ten thousand chrysanthemums', was fond of this flower.

Mangiku sat on a bulky cushion of purple silk, facing his dressing-table. 'I wonder if you'd mind telling the gentleman from Sakuragi Street?' (Mangiku, in the old-fashioned manner, referred to his dancing and singing teachers by the names of the streets where they lived.) 'It'd be hard for me to tell him.' He gazed directly into the mirror as he spoke. Masuyama could see from where he sat by the wall the nape of Mangiku's neck and the reflections in the the mirror of his face still made up for the part of Hinaginu. The eyes were not on Masuyama; they were squarely contemplating his own face. The flush from his exertions on the stage still glowed through the powder on his cheeks, like the morning sun through a thin sheet of ice. He was looking at Hinaginu.

Indeed, he actually saw her in the mirror – Hinaginu, whom he had just been impersonating, Hinaginu, the daughter of Mori Sanzaemon Yoshinari and the bride of the young Satō Kazuenosuke. Her marriage ties with her husband having been broken because of his feudal loyalty, Hinaginu killed herself so that she might remain faithful to a union 'whose ties were so faint we never shared the same bed'. Hinaginu had died on stage of a despair so extreme she could not bear to live any longer. The Hinaginu in the mirror was a ghost. Even that ghost, Mangiku knew, was at this very moment slipping from his body. His eyes pursued Hinaginu. But as the glow of the ardent passions of the role subsided, Hinaginu's face faded away. He bade it farewell. There were still seven performances before the final day. Tomorrow again Hinaginu's features would no doubt return to the pliant mould of Mangiku's face.

Masuyama, enjoying the sight of Mangiku in this abstracted state, all but smiled with affection. Mangiku suddenly turned towards him. He had been aware all along of Masuyama's gaze, but with the nonchalance of the actor, accustomed to the public's stares, he continued with his business. 'It's those instrumental passages. They're simply not long enough. I don't mean I can't get through the part if I hurry, but it makes everything so ugly.' Mangiku was referring to the music for the new dance-play which would be presented the following month. 'Mr Masuyama, what do *you* think?'

'I quite agree. I'm sure you mean the passage after "How slow the day ends by the Chinese bridge at Seta." '

'Yes, that's the place. How-ow slo-ow the da-ay . . .' Mangiku sang the passage in question, beating time with his delicate fingers.

'I'll tell him. I'm sure that the gentleman from Sakuragi Street will understand.'

'Are you sure you don't mind? I feel so embarrassed about making a nuisance of myself all the time.'

Mangiku was accustomed to terminate a conversation by standing, once his business had been dealt with. 'I'm afraid I must bathe now,' he said. Masuyama drew back from the narrow entrance to the dressing-room and let Mangiku pass. Mangiku, with a slight bow of the head, went out into the corridor, accompanied by a disciple. He turned back obliquely towards Masuyama and, smiling, bowed again. The rouge at the corners of his eyes had an indefinable charm. Masuyama sensed that Mangiku was well aware of his affection.

4

The troupe to which Masuyama belonged was to remain at the same theatre through November, December, and January, and the programme for January had already become the subject of gossip. A new work by a playwright of the modern theatre was to be staged. The man, whose sense of his own importance accorded poorly with his youth, had imposed innumerable conditions, and Masuyama was kept frantically busy with complicated negotiations intended to bring together not only the dramatist and the actors but the management of the theatre as well. Masuyama was recruited for this job because the others considered him to be an intellectual.

One of the conditions laid down by the playwright was that the direction of the play be confided to a talented young man whom he trusted. The management accepted this condition. Mangiku also agreed, but without enthusiasm. He conveyed his doubts in this manner: 'I don't really know, of course, but if this young man doesn't understand kabuki very well, and makes unreasonable demands on us, it will be so hard explaining.' Mangiku was hoping for an older, more mature – by which he meant a more compliant – director.

The new play was a dramatization in modern language of the twelfth-century novel *If Only I could Change Them!* The managing director of the company, deciding not to leave the production of this new work to the regular staff, announced it would be in Masuyama's hands. Masuyama grew tense at the thought of the work ahead of him but, convinced that the play was first-rate, he felt that it would be worth the trouble.

As soon as the scripts were ready and the parts assigned, a preliminary meeting was held one mid-December morning in the reception room adjoining the office of the theatre owner. The meeting was attended by the executive in charge of production, the playwright, the director, the stage designer, the actors, and Masuyama. The room was warmly heated and sunlight poured through the windows. Masuyama always felt happiest at preliminary meetings. It was like spreading out a map and discussing a projected outing: Where do we board the bus and where do we start walking? Is there drinking water where we're going? Where are we going to eat lunch? Where is the best view? Shall we take the train back? Or would it be better to allow enough time to return by boat?

Kawasaki, the director, was late. Masuyama had never seen a play directed by Kawasaki, but he knew of him by reputation. Kawasaki had been selected, despite his youth, to direct Ibsen and modern American plays for a repertory company, and in the course of a year had done so well, with the latter especially, that he was awarded a newspaper drama prize.

The others (except for Kawasaki) had all assembled. The designer, who could never bear waiting a minute before throwing himself into his work, was already jotting down in a large notebook especially brought for the purpose suggestions made by the others, frequently tapping the end of his pencil on the blank pages, as if bursting with ideas. Eventually the executive began to gossip about the absent director. 'He may be as talented as they say, but he's still young, after all. The actors will have to help out.'

At this moment there was a knock at the door and a secretary showed in Kawasaki. He entered the room with a dazed look, as if the light were too strong for him and, without uttering a word, stiffly bowed towards the others. He was rather tall, almost six feet, with deeply etched, masculine – but highly sensitive – features. It was a cold winter day, but Kawasaki wore a rumpled, thin raincoat. Underneath, as he presently disclosed, he had on a brick-coloured corduroy jacket. His long, straight hair hung down so far – to the tip of his nose – that he was frequently obliged to push it back. Masuyama was rather disappointed by his first impression. He had supposed that a man who had been singled out for his abilities would have attempted to distinguish himself somehow from the stereotypes of society, but this man dressed and acted exactly in the way one would expect of the typical young man of the modern theatre.

Kawasaki took the place offered him at the head of the table. He did not make the usual polite protests against the honour. He kept his eyes on the playwright, his close friend, and when introduced to each of the actors he uttered a word of greeting, only to turn back at once to the playwright. Masuyama could remember similar experiences. It is not easy for a man trained in the modern theatre, where most of the actors are young, to establish himself on easy terms with the kabuki actors, who are likely to prove to be imposing old gentlemen when encountered off stage.

The actors assembled for this preliminary meeting managed in fact to convey somehow their contempt for Kawasaki, all with a show of the greatest politeness and without an unfriendly word. Masuyama happened to glance at Mangiku's face. He modestly kept to himself, refraining from any demonstration of self-importance; he displayed no trace of the others' contempt. Masuyama felt greater admiration and affection than ever for Mangiku.

Now that everyone was present, the author described the play in outline. Mangiku, probably for the first time in his career – leaving aside parts he took as a child – was to play a male role. The plot told of a certain Grand Minister with two children, a boy and a girl. By nature they are quite unsuited to their sexes and are therefore reared accordingly: the boy (actually the girl) eventually becomes General of the Left, and the girl (actually the boy) becomes the chief lady-in-waiting in the Senyōden, the palace of the Imperial concubines. Later, when the truth is revealed, they revert to lives more appropriate to the sex of their birth; the brother marries the fourth daughter of the Minister of the Right, and sister a Middle Counsellor, and all ends happily.

Mangiku's part was that of the girl who is in reality a man. Although this was a male role, Mangiku would appear as a man only in the few moments of the final scene. Up to that point, he was to act throughout as a true *onnagata* in the part of a chief lady-in-waiting at the Senyōden. The author and director were agreed in urging Mangiku not to make any special attempt even in the last scene to suggest that he was in fact a man.

An amusing aspect of the play was that it inevitably had the effect of satirizing the kabuki convention of the *onnagata*. The lady-in-waiting was actually a man; so, in precisely the same manner, was Mangiku in the role. That was not all. In order for Mangiku, at once an *onnagata* and a man, to perform this part, he would have to unfold on two levels his actions of real life, a far cry from the simple case of the actor who assumes female costume during the course of a play so as to work some deception. The complexities of the part intrigued Mangiku.

Kawasaki's first words to Mangiku were, 'I would be glad if you played the part throughout as a woman. It doesn't make the least difference if you act like a woman even in the last scene.' His voice had a pleasant, clear ring.

'Really? If you don't mind my acting the part that way, it'll make it ever so much easier for me.'

'It won't be easy in any case. Definitely not,' said Kawasaki decisively. When he spoke in this forceful manner his cheeks glowed red as if a lamp had been lit inside. The sharpness of his tone cast something of a pall over the gathering. Masuyama's eyes wandered to Mangiku. He was giggling good-naturedly, the back of his hand pressed to his mouth. The others relaxed to see Mangiku had not been offended.

'Well, then,' said the author, 'I shall read the book.' He lowered his protruding eyes, which looked double behind his thick spectacles, and began to read the script on the table.

5

Two or three days later the rehearsal by parts began, whenever the different actors had free time. Full-scale rehearsals would only be possible during the few days in between the end of this month and the beginning of next month's programme. Unless everything that needed tightening were attended to by then, there would be no time to pull the performance together.

Once the rehearsal of the parts began it became apparent to everyone that Kawasaki was like a foreigner strayed among them. He had not the smallest grasp of kabuki, and Masuyama found himself obliged to stand beside him and explain word by word the technical language of the kabuki theatre, making Kawasaki extremely dependent on him. The instant the first rehearsal was over Masuyama invited Kawasaki for a drink.

Masuyama knew that for someone in his position it was generally speaking a mistake to ally himself with the director, but he felt he could easily understand what Kawasaki must be experiencing. The young man's views were precisely defined, his mental attitudes were wholesome, and he threw himself into his work with boyish enthusiasm. Masuyama could see why Kawasaki's character should have so appealed to the playwright; he felt as if Kawasaki's genuine youthfulness were a somehow purifying element, a quality unknown in the world of kabuki. Masuyama justified his friendship with Kawasaki in terms of attempting to turn this quality to the advantage of kabuki.

Full-scale rehearsals began at last on the day after the final performances of the December programme. It was two days after Christmas. The year-end excitement in the streets could be sensed even through the windows in the theatre and the dressing-rooms. A battered old desk had been placed by a window in the large rehearsal room. Kawasaki and one of Masuyama's seniors on the staff – the stage manager – sat with their backs to the window. Masuyama was behind Kawasaki. The authors sat on the *tatami* along the wall. Each would go up centre when his turn came to recite his lines. The stage manager supplied forgotten lines.

Sparks flew repeatedly between Kawasaki and the actors. 'At this point,' Kawasaki would say, 'I'd like you to stand as you say, "I wish I could go to Kawachi and have done with it." Then you're to walk up to the pillar at stage right.'

'That's one place I simply can't stand up.'

'Please try doing it my way.' Kawasaki forced a smile, but his face visibly paled with wounded pride.

'You can ask me to stand up from now until next Christmas, but I still can't do it. I'm supposed at this place to be mulling over something. How can I walk across stage when I'm thinking?'

Kawasaki did not answer, but he betrayed his extreme irritation at being addressed in such terms.

But things were quite different when it came to Mangiku's turn. If Kawasaki said, 'Sit!' Mangiku would sit, and if he said 'Stand!' Mangiku stood. He obeyed unresistingly every direction given by Kawasaki. It seemed to Masuyama that Mangiku's fondness for the part did not fully explain why he was so much more obliging than was his custom at rehearsals.

Masuyama was forced to leave this rehearsal on business just as Mangiku, having run through his scene in the first act, was returning to his seat by the wall. When Masuyama got back, he was met by the following sight: Kawasaki, all but sprawled over the desk, was intently following the rehearsal, not bothering even to push back the long hair falling over his eyes. He was leaning on his crossed arms, the shoulders beneath the corduroy jacket shaking with suppressed rage. To Masuyama's right was a white wall interrupted by a window, through which he could see a balloon swaying in the northerly wind, its streamer proclaiming an end-of-the-year sale. Hard, wintry clouds looked as if they had been blocked in with chalk against the pale blue of the sky. He noticed a shrine to Inari and a tiny vermilion torii on the roof of an old building near by. Farther to his right, by the wall, Mangiku sat erect in Japanese style on the *tatami*. The script lay open on his lap, and the lines of his greenish-grey kimono were perfectly straight. From where Masuyama stood at the door he could not see Mangiku's full face; but the eyes, seen in profile, were utterly tranquil, the gentle gaze fixed unwaveringly on Kawasaki.

Masuyama felt a momentary shudder of fear. He had set one foot inside the rehearsal room, but it was now almost impossible to go in.

6

Later in the day Masuyama was summoned to Mangiku's dressing-room. He felt an unaccustomed emotional block when he bent his head, as so often before, to pass through the door curtains. Mangiku greeted him, all smiles, from his perch on the purple cushion and offered Masuyama some cakes he had been given by a visitor.

'How do you think the rehearsal went today?'

'Pardon me?' Masuyama was startled by the question. It was not like Mangiku to ask his opinion on such matters.

'How did it seem?'

'If everything continues to go as well as it did today, I think the play'll be a hit.'

'Do you really think so? I feel terribly sorry for Mr Kawasaki. It's so hard for him. The others have been treating him in such a high-handed way that it's made me quite nervous. I'm sure you could tell from the rehearsal that I've made up my mind to play the part exactly as Mr Kawasaki says. That's the way I'd like to play it myself anyway, and I thought it might make things a little easier for Mr Kawasaki, even if nobody else helps. I can't very well tell the others, but I'm sure they'll notice if I do exactly what I'm told. They know how difficult I usually am. That's the least I can do to protect Mr Kawasaki. It'd be a shame, when he's trying so hard, if nobody helped.'

Masuyama felt no particular surge of emotions as he listened to Mangiku. Quite likely, he thought, Mangiku himself was unaware that he was in love: he was so accustomed to portraying love on a more heroic scale. Masuyama, for his part, considered that these sentiments – however they were to be termed – which had formed in Mangiku's heart were most inappropriate. He expected of Mangiku a far more transparent, artificial, aesthetic display of emotions.

Mangiku, most unusually for him, sat rather informally, imparting a kind of languor to his delicate figure. The mirror reflected the cluster of crimson asters arranged in the cloisonné vase and the recently shaved nape of Mangiku's neck.

Kawasaki's exasperation had become pathetic by the day before stage rehearsals began. As soon as the last private rehearsal ended, he invited Masuyama for a drink, looking as if he had reached the end of his tether. Masuyama was busy at the moment, but two hours later he found Kawasaki in the bar where they had arranged to meet, still waiting for him. The bar was crowded, though it was the night before New Year's Eve, when bars are usually deserted. Kawasaki's face looked pale as he sat drinking alone. He was the kind who only gets paler the more he has had to drink. Masuyama, catching sight of Kawasaki's ashen face as soon as he entered the bar, felt that the young man had saddled him with an unfairly heavy spiritual burden. They lived in different worlds; there was no reason why courtesy should demand that Kawasaki's uncertainties and anguish should fall so squarely on his shoulders.

Kawasaki, as he rather expected, immediately engaged him with a good-natured taunt, accusing him of being a double agent. Masuyama took the charge with a smile. He was only five or six years older than Kawasaki, but he possessed the self-confidence of a man who had dwelt among people who 'knew the score'. At the same time, he felt a kind of envy of this man who had never known hardship, or at any rate, enough hardship. It was not exactly a lack of moral integrity which had made Masuyama indifferent to most of the backstage gossip directed against him, now that he was securely placed in the kabuki hierarchy; his indifference demonstrated that he had nothing to do with the kind of sincerity which might destroy him.

Kawasaki spoke. 'I'm fed up with the whole thing. Once the curtain goes up on opening night, I'll be only too glad to disappear from the picture. Stage rehearsals beginning tomorrow! That's more than I can take, when I'm feeling so disgusted. This is the worst assignment I've ever had. I've reached my limit. Never again will I barge into a world that's not my own.'

'But isn't that what you more or less expected from the outset? Kabuki's not the same as the modern theatre, after all.' Masuyama's voice was cold.

Kawasaki's next words came as a surprise. 'Mangiku's the

hardest to take. I really dislike him. I'll never stage another play with him.' Kawasaki stared at the curling wisps of smoke under the low ceiling, as if into the face of an invisible enemy.

'I wouldn't have guessed it. It seems to me he's doing his best to be cooperative.'

'What makes you think so? What's so good about him? It doesn't bother me too much when the other actors don't listen to me during rehearsals or try to intimidate me, or even when they sabotage the whole works, but Mangiku's more than I can figure out. All he does is stare at me with that sneer on his face. At bottom he's absolutely uncompromising, and he treats me like an ignorant little squirt. That's why he does everything exactly as I say. He's the only one of them who obeys my directions, and that burns me up all the more. I can tell just what he's thinking: "If that's the way you want it, that's the way I'll do it, but don't expect me to take any responsibility for what happens in the performance." That's what he keeps flashing at me, without saying a word, and it's the worst sabotage I know. He's the nastiest of the lot.'

Masuyama listened in astonishment, but he shrank from revealing the truth to Kawasaki now. He hesitated even to let Kawasaki know that Mangiku was intending to be friendly, much less the whole truth. Kawasaki was baffled as to how he should respond to the entirely unfamiliar emotions of this world into which he had suddenly plunged; if he were informed of Mangiku's feelings, he might easily suppose they represented just one more snare laid for him. His eyes were too clear: for all his grasp of the principles of theatre, he could not detect the dark, aesthetic presence lurking behind the texts.

The New Year came and with it the first night of the new programme.

Mangiku was in love. His sharp-eyed disciples were the first to gossip about it. Masuyama, a frequent visitor to Mangiku's dressing-room, sensed it in the atmosphere almost immediately. Mangiku was wrapped in his love like a silkworm in its cocoon, soon to emerge as a butterfly. His dressing-room was the cocoon of his love. Mangiku was of a retiring disposition in any case, but the contrast with the New Year's excitement elsewhere gave his dressing-room a peculiarly solemn hush.

On the opening night, Masuyama, noticing as he passed Mangiku's dressing-room that the door was wide open, decided to take a look inside. He saw Mangiku from behind, seated before the mirror in full costume, waiting for his signal to go on. His eyes took in the pale lavender of Mangiku's robe, the gentle slope of the powdered and half-exposed shoulders, the glossy, lacquer-black wig. Mangiku at such moments in the deserted dressing-room looked like a woman absorbed in her spinning; she was spinning her love, and would continue spinning for ever, her mind elsewhere.

Masuyama intuitively understood that the mould for this *onnagata*'s love had been provided by the stage alone. The stage was present all day long, the stage where love was incessantly shouting, grieving, shedding blood. Music celebrating the sublime heights of love sounded perpetually in Mangiku's ears, and each exquisite gesture of his body was constantly employed on stage for the purpose of love. To the tips of his fingers, nothing about Mangiku was alien to love. His toes encased in white *tabi*, the seductive colours of his under kimono barely glimpsed through the openings in his sleeves, the long, swanlike nape of his neck were all in the service of love.

Masuyama did not doubt but that Mangiku would obtain guidance in pursuing his love from the grandiose emotions of his stage roles. The ordinary actor is apt to enrich his performances by infusing them with the emotions of his real life, but not Mangiku. The instant that Mangiku fell in love, the loves of Yukihime, Omiwa, Hinaginu, and the other tragic heroines came to his support.

The thought of Mangiku in love took Masuyama aback, however. Those tragic emotions for which he had yearned so fervently since his days as a high-school student, those sublime emotions which Mangiku always evoked through his corporeal presence on stage, encasing his sensual faculties in icy flames, Mangiku was now visibly nurturing in real life. But the object of these emotions – granted that he had some talent – was an ignoramus as far as kabuki was concerned; he was merely a young, commonplace-looking director whose only qualification as the object of Mangiku's love consisted in being a foreigner in this country, a young traveller who would soon depart the world of kabuki and never return.

7

If Only I Could Change Them! was well received. Kawasaki, despite his announced intention of disappearing after opening night, came to the theatre every day to complain of the performance, to rush back and forth incessantly through the subterranean passages under the stage, to finger with curiosity the mechanisms of the trap door or the *hanamichi*. Masuyama thought this man had something childish about him.

The newspaper reviews praised Mangiku. Masuyama made it a point to show them to Kawasaki, but he merely pouted, like an obstinate child, and all but spat out the words, 'They're all good at acting. But there wasn't any *direction*.' Masuyama naturally did not relay to Mangiku these harsh words, and Kawasaki himself was on his best behaviour when he actually met Mangiku. It nevertheless irritated Masuyama that Mangiku, who was utterly blind when it came to other people's feelings, should not have questioned that Kawasaki was aware of his good will. But Kawasaki was absolutely insensitive to what other people might feel. This was the one trait that Kawasaki and Mangiku had in common.

A week after the first performance Masuyama was summoned to Mangiku's dressing-room. Mangiku displayed on his table amulets and charms from the shrine where he regularly worshipped, as well as some small New Year's cakes. The cakes would no doubt be distributed later among his disciples. Mangiku pressed some sweets on Masuyama, a sign that he was in a good mood. 'Mr Kawasaki was here a little while ago,' he said.

'Yes, I saw him out front.'

'I wonder if he's still in the theatre.'

'I imagine he'll stay until *If Only* is over.'

'Did he say anything about being busy afterwards?'

'No, nothing particular.'

'Then, I have a little favour I'd like to ask you.'

Masuyama assumed as businesslike an expression as he could muster. 'What might it be?'

'Tonight, you see, when the performance is over . . . I mean, tonight . . .' The colour had mounted in Mangiku's cheeks. His voice was clearer and higher-pitched than usual. 'Tonight, when the performance is over, I thought I'd like to have dinner with him. Would you mind asking if he's free?'

'I'll ask him.'

'It's dreadful of me, isn't it, to ask you such a thing.'

'That's quite all right.' Masuyama sensed that Mangiku's eyes at that moment had stopped roving and were trying to read his expression. He seemed to expect – and even to desire – some perturbation on Masuyama's part. 'Very well,' Masuyama said, rising at once, 'I'll inform him.'

Hardly had Masuyama gone into the lobby than he ran into Kawasaki, coming from the opposite direction; this chance meeting amidst the crowd thronging the lobby during the interval seemed like a stroke of fate. Kawasaki's manner poorly accorded with the festive air pervading the lobby. The somehow haughty airs which the young man always adopted seemed rather comic when set amidst a buzzing crowd of solid citizens dressed in holiday finery and attending the theatre merely for the pleasure of seeing a play.

Masuyama led Kawasaki to a corner of the lobby and informed him of Mangiku's request.

'I wonder what he wants with me now? Dinner together – that's funny. I have nothing else to do tonight, and there's no reason why I can't go, but I don't see why.'

'I suppose there's something he wants to discuss about the play.'

'The play! I've said all I want to on that subject.'

At this moment a gratuitous desire to do evil, an emotion always associated on the stage with minor villains, took seed within Masuyama's heart, though he did not realize it; he was not aware that he himself was now acting like a character in a play. 'Don't you see – being invited to dinner gives you a marvellous opportunity to tell him everything you've got on your mind, this time without mincing words.'

'All the same – '

'I don't suppose you've got the nerve to tell him.'

The remark wounded the young man's pride. 'All right. I'll go. I've known all along that sooner or later I'd have my chance to have it out with him in the open. Please tell him that I'm glad to accept his invitation.'

Mangiku appeared in the last work of the programme and was not free until the entire performance was over. Once the show ends, actors normally make a quick change of clothes and rush from the theatre, but Mangiku showed no sign of haste as he completed his dressing by putting a cape and a scarf of a muted colour over his outer kimono. He waited for Kawasaki. When Kawasaki at last appeared, he curtly greeted Mangiku, not bothering to take his hands from his overcoat pockets.

The disciple who always waited on Mangiku as his 'lady's maid' rushed up, as if to announce some major calamity. 'It's started to snow,' he reported with a bow.

'A heavy snow?' Mangiku touched his cape to his cheek.

'No, just a flurry.'

'We'll need an umbrella to the car,' Mangiku said. The disciple rushed off for an umbrella.

Masuyama saw them to the stage entrance. The door attendant had politely arranged Mangiku's and Kawasaki's footwear next to each other. Mangiku's disciple stood outside in the thin snow, holding an open umbrella. The snow fell so sparsely that one couldn't be sure one saw it against the dark concrete wall beyond. One or two flakes fluttered on to the doorstep at the stage entrance.

Mangiku bowed to Masuyama. 'We'll be leaving now,' he said. The smile on his lips could be seen indistinctly behind his scarf. He turned to the disciple, 'That's all right. I'll carry the umbrella. I'd like you to go instead and tell the driver we're ready.' Mangiku held the umbrella over Kawasaki's head. As Kawasaki in his overcoat and Mangiku in his cape walked off side by side under the umbrella, a few flakes suddenly flew – all but bounced – from the umbrella.

Masuyama watched them go. He felt as though a big, black wet umbrella were being noisily opened inside his heart. He could tell that the illusion, first formed when as a boy he saw Mangiku perform, an illusion which he had preserved intact even after he joined the kabuki staff, had shattered that instant in all directions, like a delicate piece of crystal dropped from a height. At last I know what disillusion means, he thought. I might as well give up the theatre.

But Masuyama knew that along with disillusion a new sensation was assaulting him, jealousy. He dreaded where this new emotion might lead him.

Translated by Donald Keene

The Pearl

December 10 was Mrs Sasaki's birthday, but since it was Mrs Sasaki's wish to celebrate the occasion with the minimum of fuss, she had invited to her house for afternoon tea only her closest friends. Assembled were Mesdames Yamamoto, Matsumura, Azuma, and Kasuga – all four being forty-three years of age, exact contemporaries of their hostess.

These ladies were thus members, as it were, of a Keep-Our-Ages-Secret Society, and could be trusted implicitly not to divulge to outsiders the number of candles on today's cake. In inviting to her birthday party only guests of this nature Mrs Sasaki was showing her customary prudence.

On this occasion Mrs Sasaki wore a pearl ring. Diamonds at an all-female gathering had not seemed in the best of taste. Furthermore, pearls better matched the colour of the dress she was wearing on this particular day.

Shortly after the party had begun, Mrs Sasaki was moving across for one last inspection of the cake when the pearl in her ring, already a little loose, finally fell from its socket. It seemed a most inauspicious event for this happy occasion, but it would have been no less embarrassing to have everyone aware of the misfortune, so Mrs Sasaki simply left the pearl close by the rim of the large cake dish and resolved to do something about it later. Around the cake were set out the plates, forks, and paper napkins for herself and the four guests. It now occurred to Mrs Sasaki that she had no wish to be seen wearing a ring with no stone while cutting this cake, and accordingly she removed the ring from her finger and very deftly, without turning round, slipped it into a recess in the wall behind her back.

Amid the general excitement of the exchange of gossip, and

Mrs Sasaki's surprise and pleasure at the thoughtful presents brought by her guests, the matter of the pearl was very quickly forgotten. Before long it was time for the customary ceremony of lighting and extinguishing the candles on the cake. Everyone crowded excitedly about the table, lending a hand in the not untroublesome task of lighting forty-three candles.

Mrs Sasaki, with her limited lung capacity, could hardly be expected to blow out all that number at one puff, and her appearance of utter helplessness gave rise to a great deal of hilarious comment.

The procedure followed in serving the cake was that, after the first bold cut, Mrs Sasaki carved for each guest individually a slice of whatever thickness was requested and transferred this to a small plate, which the guest then carried back with her to her own seat. With everyone stretching out hands at the same time, the crush and confusion around the table was considerable.

On top of the cake was a floral design executed in pink icing and liberally interspersed with small silver balls. These were silver-painted crystals of sugar – a common enough decoration on birthday cakes. In the struggle to secure helpings, moreover, flakes of icing, crumbs of cake, and a number of these silver balls came to be scattered all over the white tablecloth. Some of the guests gathered these stray particles between their fingers and put them on their plates. Others popped them straight into their mouths.

In time all returned to their seats and ate their portions of cake at their leisure, laughing. It was not a home-made cake, having been ordered by Mrs Sasaki from a certain high-class confectioner's, but the guests were unanimous in praising its excellence.

Mrs Sasaki was bathed in happiness. But suddenly, with a tinge of anxiety, she recalled the pearl she had abandoned on the table, and, rising from her chair as casually as she could, she moved across to look for it. At the spot where she was sure she had left it, the pearl was no longer to be seen.

Mrs Sasaki abhorred losing things. At once and without

thinking, right in the middle of the party, she became wholly engrossed in her search, and the tension in her manner was so obvious that it attracted everyone's attention.

'Is there something the matter?' someone asked.

'No, not at all, just a moment . . .'

Mrs Sasaki's reply was ambiguous, but before she had time to decide to return to her chair, first one, then another, and finally every one of her guests had risen and was turning back the tablecloth or groping about on the floor.

Mrs Azuma, seeing this commotion, felt that the whole thing was just too deplorable for words. She was incensed at a hostess who could create such an impossible situation over the loss of a solitary pearl.

Mrs Azuma resolved to offer herself as a sacrifice and to save the day. With a heroic smile she declared: 'That's it then! It must have been a pearl I ate just now! A silver ball dropped on the tablecloth when I was given my cake, and I just picked it up and swallowed it without thinking. It *did* seem to stick in my throat a little. Had it been a diamond, now, I would naturally return it – by an operation, if necessary – but as it's a pearl I must simply beg your forgiveness.'

This announcement at once resolved the company's anxieties, and it was felt, above all, that it had saved the hostess from an embarrassing predicament. No one made any attempt to investigate the truth or falsity of Mrs Azuma's confession. Mrs. Sasaki took one of the remaining silver balls and put it in her mouth.

'Mm,' she said. 'Certainly tastes like a pearl, this one!'

Thus this small incident, too, was cast into the crucible of good-humoured teasing, and there – amid general laughter – it melted away.

When the party was over Mrs Azuma drove off in her two-seater sports car, taking with her in the other seat her close friend and neighbour Mrs Kasuga. Before two minutes had passed Mrs Azuma said, 'Own up! It was you who swallowed the pearl, wasn't it? I covered up for you, and took the blame on myself.'

This unceremonious manner of speaking concealed deep

affection, but, however friendly the intention may have been, to Mrs Kasuga a wrongful accusation was a wrongful accusation. She had no recollection whatsoever of having swallowed a pearl in mistake for a sugar ball. She was – as Mrs Azuma too must surely know – fastidious in her eating habits, and, if she so much as detected a single hair in her food, whatever she happened to be eating at the time immediately stuck in her gullet.

'Oh, really now!' protested the timid Mrs Kasuga, in a small voice, her eyes studying Mrs Azuma's face in some puzzlement. 'I just couldn't do a thing like that!'

'It's no good pretending. The moment I saw that green look on your face, I knew.'

The little disturbance at the party had seemed closed by Mrs Azuma's frank confession, but even now it had left behind this strange awkwardness. Mrs Kasuga, wondering how best to demonstrate her innocence, was at the same time seized by the fantasy that a solitary pearl was lodged somewhere in her intestines. It was unlikely, of course, that she should mistakenly swallow a pearl for a sugar ball, but in all that confusion of talk and laughter one had to admit that it was at least a possibility. Though she thought back over the events of the party again and again, no moment in which she might have inserted a pearl into her mouth came to mind – but, after all, if it was an unconscious act one would not expect to remember it.

Mrs Kasuga blushed deeply as her imagination chanced upon one further aspect of the matter. It had occurred to her that when one accepted a pearl into one's system it almost certainly – its lustre a trifle dimmed, perhaps, by gastric juices – re-emerged intact within a day or two.

And with this thought the design of Mrs Azuma, too, seemed to have become transparently clear. Undoubtedly Mrs Azuma had viewed this same prospect with embarrassment and shame, and had therefore cast her responsibility on to another, making it appear that she had considerately taken the blame to protect a friend.

Meanwhile Mrs Yamamoto and Mrs Matsumura, whose homes lay in a similar direction, were returning together in a taxi. Soon after the taxi had started Mrs Matsumura opened her handbag to make a few adjustments to her make-up. She remembered that she had done nothing to her face since all that commotion at the party.

As she was removing the powder compact her attention was caught by a sudden dull gleam as something tumbled to the bottom of the bag. Groping about with the tips of her fingers, Mrs Matsumura retrieved the object, and saw to her amazement that it was a pearl.

Mrs Matsumura stifled an exclamation of surprise. Recently her relationship with Mrs Yamamoto had been far from cordial, and she had no wish to share with that lady a discovery with such awkward implications for herself.

Fortunately Mrs Yamamoto was gazing out of the window and did not appear to have noticed her companion's momentary start of surprise.

Caught off balance by this sudden turn of events, Mrs Matsumura did not pause to consider how the pearl had found its way into her bag, but immediately became a prisoner of her own private brand of school-captain morality. It was unlikely – she thought – that she would do a thing like this, even in a moment of abstraction. But since, by some chance, the object had found its way into her handbag, the proper course was to return it at once. If she failed to do so, it would weigh heavily upon her conscience. The fact that it was a pearl, too – an article you could neither call all that expensive nor yet all that cheap – only made her position more ambiguous.

At any rate, she was determined that her companion, Mrs Yamamoto, should know nothing of this incomprehensible development – especially when the affair had been so nicely rounded off, thanks to the selflessness of Mrs Azuma. Mrs Matsumura felt she could remain in the taxi not a moment longer, and, on the pretext of remembering a promise to visit a sick relative on her way back, she made the driver set her down at once, in the middle of a quiet residential district.

Mrs Yamamoto, left alone in the taxi, was a little surprised that her practical joke should have moved Mrs. Matsumura to such abrupt action. Having watched Mrs Matsumura's reflection in the window just now, she had clearly seen her draw the pearl from her bag.

At the party Mrs Yamamoto had been the very first to receive a slice of cake. Adding to her plate a silver ball which had spilled on to the table, she had returned to her seat – again before any of the others – and there had noticed that the silver ball was a pearl. At this discovery she had at once conceived a malicious plan. While all the others were preoccupied with the cake, she had quickly slipped the pearl into the handbag left on the next chair by that insufferable hypocrite Mrs Matsumura.

Stranded in the middle of a residential district where there was little prospect of a taxi, Mrs Matsumura fretfully gave her mind to a number of reflections on her position.

First, no matter how necessary it might be for the relief of her own conscience, it would be a shame indeed, when people had gone to such lengths to settle the affairs satisfactorily, to go and stir up things all over again; and it would be even worse if in the process – because of the inexplicable nature of the circumstances – she were to direct unjust suspicions upon herself.

Secondly – notwithstanding these considerations – if she did not make haste to return the pearl now, she would forfeit her opportunity for ever. Left till tomorrow (at the thought Mrs Matsumura blushed) the returned pearl would be an object of rather disgusting speculation and doubt. Concerning this possibility Mrs Azuma herself had dropped a hint.

It was at this point that there occurred to Mrs Matsumura, greatly to her joy, a master scheme which would both salve her conscience and at the same time involve no risk of exposing her character to any unjust suspicion. Quickening her step, she emerged at length on to a comparatively busy thoroughfare, where she hailed a taxi and told the driver to take her quickly to a certain celebrated pearl shop on the Ginza. There she took the pearl from her bag and showed it to the attendant, asking to see a pearl of slightly larger size and clearly superior quality. Having made her purchase, she proceeded once more, by taxi, to Mrs Sasaki's house.

Mrs Matsumura's plan was to present this newly purchased

pearl to Mrs Sasaki, saying that she had found it in her jacket pocket. Mrs Sasaki would accept it and later attempt to fit it into the ring. However, being a pearl of a different size, it would not fit into the ring, and Mrs Sasaki – puzzled – would try to return it to Mrs Matsumura, but Mrs Matsumura would refuse to have it returned. Thereupon Mrs Sasaki would have no choice but to reflect as follows: The woman has behaved in this way in order to protect someone else. Such being the case, it is perhaps safest simply to accept the pearl and forget the matter. Mrs Matsumura has doubtless observed one of the three ladies in the act of stealing the pearl. But at least, of my four guests, I can now be sure that Mrs Matsumura, if no one else, is completely without guilt. Whoever heard of a thief stealing something and then replacing it with a similar article of greater value?

By this device Mrs Matsumura proposed to escape for ever the infamy of suspicion, and equally – by a small outlay of cash – the pricks of an uneasy conscience.

To return to the other ladies. After reaching home, Mrs Kasuga continued to feel painfully upset by Mrs Azuma's cruel teasing. To clear herself of even a ridiculous charge like this – she knew – she must act before tomorrow or it would be too late. That is to say, in order to offer positive proof that she had not eaten the pearl it was above all necessary for the pearl itself to be somehow produced. And, briefly, if she could show the pearl to Mrs Azuma immediately, her innocence on the gastronomic count (if not on any other) would be firmly established. But if she waited until tomorrow, even though she managed to produce the pearl, the shameful and hardly mentionable suspicion would inevitably have intervened.

The normally timid Mrs Kasuga, inspired with the courage of impetuous action, burst from the house to which she had so recently returned, sped to a pearl shop in the Ginza, and selected and bought a pearl which, to her eye, seemed of roughly the same size as those silver balls on the cake. She then telephoned Mrs Azuma. On returning home, she explained, she had discovered in the folds of the bow of her sash the pearl which Mrs

Sasaki had lost, but, since she felt too ashamed to return it by herself, she wondered if Mrs Azuma would be so kind as to go with her, as soon as possible. Inwardly Mrs Azuma considered the story a little unlikely, but since it was the request of a good friend she agreed to go.

Mrs Sasaki accepted the pearl brought to her by Mrs Matsumura and, puzzled at its failure to fit the ring, fell obligingly into that very train of thought for which Mrs Matsumura had prayed; but it was a surprise to her when Mrs Kasuga arrived about an hour later, accompanied by Mrs Azuma, and returned another pearl.

Mrs Sasaki hovered perilously on the brink of discussing Mrs Matsumura's prior visit, but checked herself at the last moment and accepted the second pearl as unconcernedly as she could. She felt sure that this one at any rate would fit, and as soon as the two visitors had taken their leave she hurried to try it in the ring. But it was too small, and wobbled loosely in the socket. At this discovery Mrs Sasaki was not so much surprised as dumbfounded.

On the way back in the car both ladies found it impossible to guess what the other might be thinking, and, though normally relaxed and loquacious in each other's company, they now lapsed into a long silence.

Mrs Azuma, who believed she could do nothing without her own full knowledge, knew for certain that she had not swallowed the pearl herself. It was simply to save everyone from embarrassment that she had cast shame aside and made that declaration at the party – more particularly it was to save the situation for her friend, who had been fidgeting about and looking conspicuously guilty. But what was she to think now? Beneath the peculiarity of Mrs Kasuga's whole attitude, and beneath this elaborate procedure of having herself accompany her as she returned the pearl, she sensed that there lay something much deeper. Could it be that Mrs Azuma's intuition had touched upon a weakness in her friend's make-up which it was forbidden to touch upon, and that by thus driving her friend into a corner she had transformed an unconscious, impulsive kleptomania into a deep mental derangement beyond all cure?

Mrs Kasuga, for her part, still retained the suspicion that Mrs Azuma had genuinely swallowed the pearl and that her confession at the party had been the truth. If that was so, it had been unforgivable of Mrs Azuma, when everything was smoothly settled, to tease her so cruelly on the way back from the party, shifting the guilt on to herself. As a result, timid creature that she was, she had been panic-stricken, and besides spending good money had felt obliged to act out that little play – and was it not exceedingly ill-natured of Mrs Azuma, that, even after all this, she still refused to confess it was she who had eaten the pearl? And if Mrs Azuma's innocence was all pretence, she herself – acting her part so painstakingly – must appear in Mrs Azuma's eyes as the most ridiculous of third-rate comedians.

To return to Mrs Matsumura. That lady, on her way back from obliging Mrs Sasaki to accept the pearl, was feeling now more at ease in her mind and had the notion to make a leisurely reinvestigation, detail by detail, of the events of the recent incident. When going to collect her portion of cake, she had most certainly left her handbag on the chair. Then, while eating the cake, she had made liberal use of the paper napkin – so there could have been no necessity to take a handkerchief from her bag. The more she thought about it the less she could remember having opened her bag until she touched up her face in the taxi on the way home. How was it, then, that a pearl had rolled into a handbag which was always shut?

She realized now how stupid she had been not to have remarked this simple fact before, instead of flying into a panic at the mere sight of the pearl. Having progressed this far, Mrs Matsumura was struck by an amazing thought. Someone must purposely have placed the pearl in her bag in order to incriminate her. And of the four guests at the party the only one who would do such a thing was, without doubt, the detestable Mrs Yamamoto. Her eyes glinting with rage, Mrs Matsumura hurried towards the house of Mrs Yamamoto.

From her first glimpse of Mrs Matsumura standing in the

doorway, Mrs Yamamoto knew at once what had brought her. She had already prepared her line of defence.

However, Mrs Matsumura's cross-examination was unexpectedly severe, and from the start it was clear that she would accept no evasions.

'It was you, I know. No one but you could do such a thing,' began Mrs Matsumura, deductively.

'Why choose me? What proof have you? If you can say a thing like that to my face, I suppose you've come with pretty conclusive proof, have you?' Mrs Yamamoto was at first icily composed.

To this Mrs Matsumura replied that Mrs Azuma, having so nobly taken the blame on herself, clearly stood in an incompatible relationship with mean and despicable behaviour of this nature; and as for Mrs Kasuga, she was much too weak-kneed for such dangerous work; and that left only one person – yourself.

Mrs Yamamoto kept silent, her mouth shut tight like a clamshell. On the table before her gleamed the pearl which Mrs Matsumura had set there. In the excitement she had not even had time to raise a teaspoon, and the Ceylon tea she had so thoughtfully provided was beginning to get cold.

'I had no idea you hated me so.' As she said this, Mrs Yamamoto dabbed at the corners of her eyes, but it was plain that Mrs Matsumura's resolve not to be deceived by tears was as firm as ever.

'Well, then,' Mrs Yamamoto continued, 'I shall say what I had thought I must never say. I shall mention no names, but one of the guests ...'

'By that, I suppose, you can only mean Mrs Azuma or Mrs Kasuga?'

'Please, I beg at least that you allow me to omit the name. As I say, one of the guests had just opened your bag and was dropping something inside when I happened to glance in her direction. You can imagine my amazement! Even if I had felt *able* to warn you, there would have been no chance. My heart just throbbed and throbbed, and on the way back in the taxi – oh, how awful not to be able to speak even then! If we had been good friends, of course, I could have told you quite frankly, but since I knew of your apparent dislike for me . . .'

'I see. You have been very considerate, I'm sure. Which means, doesn't it, that you have now cleverly shifted the blame on to Mrs Azuma and Mrs Kasuga?'

'Shifted the blame? Oh, how can I get you to understand my feelings? I only wanted to avoid hurting anyone.'

'Quite. But you didn't mind hurting me, did you? You might at least have mentioned this in the taxi.'

'And if you had been frank with me when you found the pearl in your bag. I would probably have told you, at that moment, everything I had seen – but no, you chose to leave the taxi at once, without saying a word!'

'Well, then. Can I get you to understand? I wanted no one to be hurt.'

Mrs Matsumura was filled with an even more intense rage.

'If you are going to tell a string of lies like that,' she said, 'I must ask you to repeat them, tonight if you wish, in my presence, before Mrs Azuma and Mrs Kasuga.'

At this Mrs Yamamoto started to weep.

'And thanks to you,' she sobbed reprovingly, 'all my efforts to avoid hurting anyone will have come to nothing.'

It was a new experience for Mrs Matsumura to see Mrs Yamamoto crying, and, though she kept reminding herself not to be taken in by tears, she could not altogether dismiss the feeling that perhaps somewhere, since nothing in this affair could be proved, there might be a modicum of truth even in the assertions of Mrs Yamamoto.

In the first place – to be a little more objective – if one accepted Mrs Yamamoto's story as true, then her reluctance to disclose the name of the guilty party, whom she had observed in the very act, argued some refinement of character. And just as one could not say for sure that the gentle and seemingly timid Mrs Kasuga would never be moved to an act of malice, so even the undoubtedly bad feeling between Mrs Yamamoto and herself could, by one way of looking at things, be taken as actually lessening the likelihood of Mrs Yamamoto's guilt. For if she were to do a thing like this, with their relationship as it was, Mrs Yamamoto would be the first to come under suspicion.

'We have differences in our natures,' Mrs Yamamoto continued tearfully, 'and I cannot deny that there are things about yourself which I dislike. But, for all that, it is really too bad that you should suspect me of such a petty trick to get the better of you. . . . Still, on thinking it over, to submit quietly to your accusations might well be the course most consistent with what I have felt in this matter all along. In this way I alone shall bear the guilt, and no other will be hurt.'

After this pathetic pronouncement Mrs Yamamoto lowered her face to the table and abandoned herself to uncontrolled weeping.

Watching her, Mrs Matsumura came by degrees to reflect upon the impulsiveness of her own behaviour. Detesting Mrs Yamamoto as she had, there had been times in her castigation of that lady when she had allowed herself to be blinded by emotion.

When Mrs Yamamoto raised her head again after this prolonged bout of weeping, the look of resolution on her face, somehow remote and pure, was apparent even to her visitor. Mrs Matsumura, a little frightened, drew herself upright in her chair.

'This thing should never have been. When it is gone, everything will be as before.' Speaking in riddles, Mrs Yamamoto pushed back her dishevelled hair and fixed a terrible, yet hauntingly beautiful gaze upon the top of the table. In an instant she had snatched up the pearl from before her, and, with a gesture of no ordinary resolve, tossed it into her mouth. Raising her cup by the handle, her little finger elegantly extended, she washed the pearl down her throat with one gulp of cold Ceylon tea.

Mrs Matsumura watched in horrified fascination. The affair was over before she had time to protest. This was the first time in her life she had seen a person swallow a pearl, and there was in Mrs Yamamoto's manner something of that desperate finality one might expect to see in a person who had just drunk poison.

However, heroic though the action was, it was above all a touching incident, and not only did Mrs Matsumura find her anger vanished into thin air, but so impressed was she by Mrs Yamamoto's simplicity and purity that she could only think of that lady as a saint. And now Mrs Matsumura's eyes too began to fill with tears, and she took Mrs Yamamoto by the hand.

'Please forgive me, please forgive me,' she said. 'It was wrong of me.'

For a while they wept together, holding each other's hands and vowing to each other that henceforth they would be the firmest of friends.

When Mrs Sasaki heard rumours that the relationship between Mrs Yamamoto and Mrs Matsumura, which had been so strained, had suddenly improved, and that Mrs Azuma and Mrs Kasuga, who had been such good friends, had suddenly fallen out, she was at a loss to understand the reasons and contented herself with the reflection that nothing was impossible in this world.

However, being a woman of no strong scruples, Mrs Sasaki requested a jeweller to refashion her ring and to produce a design into which two new pearls could be set, one large and one small, and this she wore quite openly, without further mishap.

Soon she had completely forgotten the small commotion on her birthday, and when anyone asked her age she would give the same untruthful answers as ever.

Translated by Geoffrey W. Sargent

Swaddling Clothes

He was always busy, Toshiko's husband. Even tonight he had to dash off to an appointment, leaving her to go home alone by taxi. But what else could a woman expect when she married an actor – an attractive one? No doubt she had been foolish to hope that he would spend the evenings with her. And yet he must have known how she dreaded going back to their house, unhomely with its Western-style furniture and with the bloodstains still showing on the floor.

Toshiko had been oversensitive since girlhood: that was her nature. As the result of constant worrying she never put on weight, and now, an adult woman, she looked more like a transparent picture than a creature of flesh and blood. Her delicacy of spirit was evident to her most casual acquaintance.

Earlier that evening, when she had joined her husband at a night club, she had been shocked to find him entertaining friends with an account of 'the incident'. Sitting there in his American-style suit, puffing at a cigarette, he had seemed to her almost a stranger.

'It's a fantastic story,' he was saying, gesturing flamboyantly as if in an attempt to outweigh the attractions of the dance band. 'Here this new nurse for our baby arrives from the employment agency, and the very first thing I notice about her is her stomach. It's enormous – as if she had a pillow stuck under her kimono! No wonder, I thought, for I soon saw that she could eat more than the rest of us put together. She polished off the contents of our rice bin like that. ...' He snapped his fingers. ' "Gastric dilation" – that's how she explained her girth and her appetite. Well, the day before yesterday we heard groans and moans coming from the nursery. We rushed in and found her squatting on the floor, holding her stomach in her two hands, and moaning like a cow. Next to her our baby lay in his cot, scared out of his wits and crying at the top of his lungs. A pretty scene, I can tell you!'

'So the cat was out of the bag?' suggested one of their friends, a film actor like Toshiko's husband.

'Indeed it was! And it gave me the shock of my life. You see, I'd completely swallowed that story about "gastric dilation". Well, I didn't waste any time. I rescued our good rug from the floor and spread a blanket for her to lie on. The whole time the girl was yelling like a stuck pig. By the time the doctor from the maternity clinic arrived, the baby had already been born. But our sitting-room was a pretty shambles!'

'Oh, that I'm sure of!' said another of their friends, and the whole company burst into laughter.

Toshiko was dumbfounded to hear her husband discussing the horrifying happening as though it were no more than an amusing incident which they chanced to have witnessed. She shut her eyes for a moment and all at once she saw the newborn baby lying before her: on the parquet floor the infant lay, and his frail body was wrapped in bloodstained newspapers.

Toshiko was sure that the doctor had done the whole thing out of spite. As if to emphasize his scorn for this mother who had given birth to a bastard under such sordid conditions, he had told his assistant to wrap the baby in some loose newspapers, rather than proper swaddling. This callous treatment of the newborn child had offended Toshiko. Overcoming her disgust at the entire scene, she had fetched a brand-new piece of flannel from her cupboard and, having swaddled the baby in it, had laid him carefully in an armchair.

This all had taken place in the evening after her husband had left the house. Toshiko had told him nothing of it, fearing that he would think her oversoft, oversentimental; yet the scene had engraved itself deeply in her mind. Tonight she sat silently thinking back on it, while the jazz orchestra brayed and her husband chatted cheerfully with his friends. She knew that she would never forget the sight of the baby, wrapped in stained newspapers and lying on the floor – it was a scene fit for a butcher's shop. Toshiko, whose own life had been spent in solid comfort, poignantly felt the wretchedness of the illegitimate baby.

I am the only person to have witnessed its shame, the thought occurred to her. The mother never saw her child lying there in its newspaper wrappings, and the baby itself of course didn't know. I alone shall have to preserve that terrible scene in my memory. When the baby grows up and wants to find out about his birth, there will be no one to tell him, so long as I preserve silence. How strange that I should have this feeling of guilt! After all, it was I who took him up from the floor, swathed him properly in flannel, and laid him down to sleep in the armchair.

They left the night club and Toshiko stepped into the taxi that her husband had called for her. 'Take this lady to Ushigomé,' he told the driver and shut the door from the outside. Toshiko gazed through the window at her husband's smiling face and noticed his strong, white teeth. Then she leaned back in the seat, oppressed by the knowledge that their life together was in some way too easy, too painless. It would have been difficult for her to put her thoughts into words. Through the rear window of the taxi she took a last look at her husband. He was striding along the street towards his Nash car, and soon the back of his rather garish tweed coat had blended with the figures of the passers-by.

The taxi drove off, passed down a street dotted with bars and then by a theatre, in front of which the throngs of people jostled each other on the pavement. Although the performance had only just ended, the lights had already been turned out and in the half dark outside it was depressingly obvious that the cherry blossoms decorating the front of the theatre were merely scraps of white paper.

Even if that baby should grow up in ignorance of the secret of his birth, he can never become a respectable citizen, reflected Toshiko, pursuing the same train of thoughts. Those soiled newspaper swaddling clothes will be the symbol of his entire life. But why should I keep worrying about him so much? Is it because I feel uneasy about the future of my own child? Say twenty years from now, when our boy will have grown up into a fine, carefully educated young man, one day by a quirk of fate he meets that other boy, who then will also have turned twenty. And say that the other boy, who has been sinned against, savagely stabs him with a knife . . .

It was a warm, overcast April night, but thoughts of the future made Toshiko feel cold and miserable. She shivered on the back seat of the car.

No, when the time comes I shall take my son's place, she told herself suddenly. Twenty years from now I shall be forty-three. I shall go to that young man and tell him straight out about everything – about his newspaper swaddling clothes, and about how I went and wrapped him in flannel.

The taxi ran along the dark wide road that was bordered by the park and by the Imperial Palace moat. In the distance Toshiko noticed the pinpricks of light which came from the blocks of tall office buildings.

Twenty years from now that wretched child will be in utter misery. He will be living a desolate, hopeless, poverty-stricken existence – a lonely rat. What else could happen to a baby who has had such a birth? He'll be wandering through the streets by himself, cursing his father, loathing his mother.

No doubt Toshiko derived a certain satisfaction from her sombre thoughts: she tortured herself with them without cease. The taxi approached Hanzomon and drove past the compound of the British Embassy. At that point the famous rows of cherry-trees were spread out before Toshiko in all their purity. On the spur of the moment she decided to go and view the blossoms by herself in the dark night. It was a strange decision for a timid and unadventurous young woman, but then she was in a strange state of mind and she dreaded the return home. That evening all sorts of unsettling fancies had burst open in her mind.

She crossed the wide street – a slim, solitary figure in the darkness. As a rule when she walked in the traffic Toshiko used to cling fearfully to her companion, but tonight she darted alone between the cars and a moment later had reached the long, narrow park that borders the Palace moat. Chidorigafuchi, it is called – the Abyss of the Thousand Birds.

Tonight the whole park had become a grove of blossoming cherry-trees. Under the calm cloudy sky the blossoms formed a mass of solid whiteness. The paper lanterns that hung from wires between the trees had been put out; in their place electric light bulbs, red, yellow, and green, shone dully beneath the blossoms. It was well past ten o'clock and most of the flower-viewers had gone home. As the occasional passers-by strolled through the park, they would automatically kick aside the empty bottles or crush the waste paper beneath their feet.

Newspapers, thought Toshiko, her mind going back once again to those happenings. Bloodstained newspapers. If a man were ever to hear of that piteous birth and know that it was he who had lain there, it would ruin his entire life. To think that I, a perfect stranger, should from now on have to keep such a secret – the secret of a man's whole existence . . .

Lost in these thoughts. Toshiko walked on through the park. Most of the people still remaining there were quiet couples; no one paid her any attention. She noticed two people sitting on a stone bench beside the moat, not looking at the blossoms, but gazing silently at the water. Pitch black it was, and swathed in heavy shadows. Beyond the moat the sombre forest of the Imperial Palace blocked her view. The trees reached up, to form a solid dark mass against the night sky. Toshiko walked slowly along the path beneath the blossoms hanging heavily overhead.

On a stone bench, slightly apart from the others, she noticed a pale object – not, as she had at first imagined, a pile of cherry blossoms, nor a garment forgotten by one of the visitors to the park. Only when she came closer did she see that it was a human form lying on the bench. Was it, she wondered, one of those miserable drunks often to be seen sleeping in public places? Obviously not, for the body had been systematically covered with newspapers, and it was the whiteness of those papers that had attracted Toshiko's attention. Standing by the bench, she gazed down at the sleeping figure.

It was a man in a brown jersey who lay there, curled up on layers of newspapers, other newspapers covering him. No doubt this had become his normal night residence now that spring had arrived. Toshiko gazed down at the man's dirty, unkempt hair, which in places had become hopelessly matted. As she observed the sleeping figure wrapped in its newspapers, she was inevitably reminded of the baby who had lain on the floor in its wretched swaddling clothes. The shoulder of the man's jersey rose and fell in the darkness in time with his heavy breathing.

It seemed to Toshiko that all her fears and premonitions had suddenly taken concrete form. In the darkness the man's pale forehead stood out, and it was a young forehead, though carved with the wrinkles of long poverty and hardship. His khaki trousers had been slightly pulled up; on his sockless feet he wore a pair of battered gym shoes. She could not see his face and suddenly had an overmastering desire to get one glimpse of it.

She walked to the head of the bench and looked down. The man's head was half-buried in his arms, but Toshiko could see that he was surprisingly young. She noticed the thick eyebrows and the fine bridge of his nose. His slightly open mouth was alive with youth.

But Toshiko had approached too close. In the silent night the newspaper bedding rustled, and abruptly the man opened his eyes. Seeing the young woman standing directly beside him, he raised himself with a jerk, and his eyes lit up. A second later a powerful hand reached out and seized Toshiko by her slender wrist.

She did not feel in the least afraid and made no effort to free herself. In a flash the thought had struck her, Ah, so the twenty years have already gone by! The forest of the Imperial Palace was pitch dark and utterly silent.

Translated by Ivan Morris

BY THE SAME AUTHOR

'Mishima's characters are observed with the sharpest of eyes and with maximum chill . . . a most beautiful writer of prose – clear, eloquent, visual' – *Financial Times*

Forbidden Colours

Embittered by three broken marriages and some ten unsatisfactory affairs, Shunsuké's abiding passion is revenge. His only pleasure is derived from witnessing the suffering of womankind. When he meets Yuichi, the beautiful, graceful athlete, and discovers the youth is homosexual, he sees the perfect means for the creation of infinite female misery . . .

Thirst for Love

Before her husband's death, Etsuko had already learnt that jealousy is useless if it cannot be controlled.

So when she arrived as a young widow at her late husband's family farm farm near Osaka, Etsuko resolved to hold her emotions in check, silently tolerating the nocturnal embraces of her father-in-law as she nursed a new secret passion. Jealousy, love, passion, hated – she could control them all as long as there was hope . . .

The Sailor Who Fell from Grace With the Sea

After five years of celibate widowhood, Fusako consummates her two-day relationship with Ryuji, a naval officer convinced of his glorious destiny . . . and they are spied on by Fusako's son, Norobu, a self-possessed thirteen-year-old, 'No. 3' in a sinister élite of precocious schoolboys.

The Temple of the Golden Pavilion

This novel was inspired by a real incident that took place in Kyoto in 1950, when an unhappy and unbalanced student of Zen Buddhism set fire to, and destroyed, the famous Golden Pavilion. While newspaper cuttings and reports of this tragedy provided the outline, the novel itself is executed with all Mishima's considerable power to disturb. Few novelists have explored pathology – and not simply pathology but also the dangers of religious devotion – with such terrible intimacy and precision.

and

THE SEA OF FERTILITY